The
Billion
Dollar
Dream

Also by Robert Day

where i am now (stories)
The Committee to Save the World (literary nonfiction)
The Last Cattle Drive (novel)
Speaking French in Kansas (stories)
We Should Have Come By Water (poetry)
In My Stead (novella)
Four Wheel Drive Quartet (novella)

THE BILLION DOLLAR DREAM

▲

stories
robert day

BkMk Press
University of Missouri-Kansas City

BkMk Press
University of Missouri-Kansas City
5101 Rockhill Road
Kansas City, MO 64110
www.umkc.edu/bkmk

Financial assistance for this project has been provided by the
Missouri Arts Council, a state agency.

Executive Editor: Robert Stewart
Managing Editor: Ben Furnish
Assistant Managing Editor: Cynthia Beard
Design: James Dissette
Copy Editor: Sandra Hiortdahl

BkMk Press wishes to thank Zoë Polando, Betsy Beasley, Ashley Wann,
and Alexandra Wendt.

Library of Congress Cataloging-in-Publication Data

Day, Robert
  [Short stories. Selections]
  The billion-dollar dream : stories / Robert Day.
    pages cm
  ISBN 978-1-943491-01-8 (pbk. : alk. paper)
  I. Title.
  PS3554.A966A6 2015
  813'.54--dc23
                          2015024592

ISBN 978-1-943491-01-8

Contents

Acknowledgments

"Free Writing," "Barrel Heat," "My Uncle's Poor French," *New Letters*

"Billion-Dollar Dream," "By the Light of the Silvery Moon," "We All Have Our Stories," "When the World Was Young and the Death of Bird Four," *North Dakota Quarterly*

"Sometimes It Is, Sometimes It Isn't," *Numéro Cinq*

"Stealing," *The Summerset Review*

This book is dedicated to Richard Harwood (1925-2001)
and Ted Solotaroff (1928-2008).

Flowers on the grave when they should have been on the table.

And for Kathryn Jankus Day

Preface

Among the stories in this collection, I like one better than the others. Of course, all are special to me in singular ways, including my favorite. There is a boy who writes his "What I Did Last Summer" essay without using any punctuation except the period. And a gravedigger working by the light of the moon with the love of his life singing in the High Plains wilderness beside him. Two women in two different stories beguile me in their search for themselves, a search I cannot fully understand even as their author. Others:

The madness of a bookstore manager who puts himself to sleep by dreaming of getting a billion dollars; the mystery of a mink coat that might or might not have been stolen. The smoke of passion and gunpowder drifting across twenty-some years of lost love. A dinner party that I myself attended.

As to my favorite, beyond its own singularity there is something else I cannot name.

Nor is there any way to account for my choice of the epigraph.

—Robert Day

I know but will not tell
you, Aunt Irene, why there
are soapsuds in the whiskey

~Alan Dugan, from "Elegy"

My Uncle's Poor French

Saturday Morning

When I was a boy, I lived for a year with my Uncle Bert in an apartment over the train station in the village of Lamothe-Montravel on the Dordogne River in Southwestern France, not far from Bordeaux. This was during the Korean War; my father had been called back to service (he had seen duty as a Navy pilot toward the end of World War II) and for reasons that were not clear to me at the time, my sister was taken to Oklahoma to live with my paternal grandmother, and I was flown to France to live with Uncle Bert. It was only later that I learned my mother had been deemed "unstable" by the adults in charge of our lives and that was why my sister and I were sent to our respective foster parents. I was ten at the time; my sister was eight.

I arrived in Bordeaux in late summer by plane from Paris. My father had taken leave from his naval base in California and returned to our home in the suburbs of Kansas City a few weeks before shipping out to Hawaii. After a couple of days' stay, and after my grandmother left with my sister, my father and I boarded a triple-tailed TWA Constellation for a flight to New York. My father was himself a captain of TWA Constellations, and it was this position he was foregoing to fly jets off a carrier off the coast of Korea—not unlike, now that I think of it, William Holden in *The Bridges of Toko-Ri*.

All of this seemed quite thrilling to me: my father first in this uniform, then that one. Pictures in *Life* magazine of the plane he had flown in World War II (the Navy Corsair), and then in "civilian life" the Lockheed Constellation, and now again in

Korea (the Panther). My father was a one-man flying machine for peace and war. No one in Hickory Grove Grade School had a father like mine.

I remember my father and my waving goodbye to my mother in Kansas City as we boarded the flight to New York. We were on the top of the stairs, and I remember how thin my mother looked, and I remember that she wasn't crying. For some reason, perhaps the movies you saw in those days, I always thought mothers cried when their children went off to Boy Scout camp, to visit a grandmother in Oklahoma, or to the Dordogne of southwestern France. My father and I waved. My mother did not wave.

In New York, my father confirmed the arrangements he had made with his airline friends in Paris to meet my plane at Orly and then to put me on an Air France flight to Bordeaux where my Uncle Bert was to pick me up. After that, my father walked me up the stairs onto my Paris-bound night flight to find my seat. He was wearing his Navy uniform, and the bill of his hat was trimmed with gold. Scrambled eggs, he called the design. It's what he got when he reenlisted, he said.

The captain of the plane, a friend of my father's, came down the aisle and shook hands with me. My father and the captain had some discussion about the winds aloft and the route we would take. I was told I would be allowed to visit the cockpit after the plane was airborne. Your father is quite a pilot, the captain told me. You should be proud of him. He tapped my father's "scrambled eggs" and said it was about time. Looking back, I suppose they were in the Pacific together and there was more to the story than I could ever know.

When it was time to go, my father had me follow him to the doorway where we said goodbye. He not only patted me on the sides of my shoulders—his usual way of saying hello or goodbye—but he shook my hand. That was the first time he'd done that.

Take care, he said. Then he walked down the steps, stood at the bottom for a moment, motioned for me to go back to my seat, saluted, and put both his thumbs in the air. I saluted back.

Through my seat's window I could see my father standing on the tarmac while the engines cranked up, and I could see that he could see me as well. He waved. I waved back. As the plane turned, the prop-wash caused my father to lean into the wind and hold his hat, one hand on the top, the other on the bill. It was the last time I saw him. And he was not my father.

Saturday: Late Afternoon

Uncle Bert's French was poor. I never knew exactly how long he had been in Lamothe before I got there, much less in France, but piecing it together as I grew older, he probably came back to Europe right after the war (he had been, I learned, a sergeant in an outfit that landed well after D-Day and made their way finally to Paris). Because I arrived on my uncle's doorstep, something of a foundling, the late summer of 1952, it would have been six or seven years that he had lived in France. As it would turn out, he'd live there another forty-odd years, and I suspect that the day he died he knew no more than the baguette tails and cheese rinds and dregs of the French he had during the year when we lived together.

I came to know about his bad French because, as a young boy in the Lamothe school, I learned the language quickly. By Christmas, I had become something of a discreet translator for my Uncle.

"What did he say? I've bum ears, boy," said my uncle. "A war wound. Too many 155s. Nothing serious. What'd he say?" And here Uncle Bert would take off his black beret, as if that might make it easier for him to understand.

"He said you owe him five francs," I said.

"Five francs it is. And cheap at half the francs."

Along with bad French, Uncle Bert also had the habit, à la Sancho Panza, of mixing up (and making up) aphorisms, a phenomenon I would learn both sooner and later when I'd finally get them straight for myself, at first with the help of tolerant teachers back in Kansas City, and later with the assistance of puzzled editors. Still: "Eating your cake and having it too" is forever tangled, while "a day short and a dollar late" I rearranged by myself not long after I heard my uncle use it. But I never knew what he had mangled when he'd say: "The road of the mind is a twisted branch." Or: "Don't feed the staff of life to an ugly pig." Or: "Flowing beer gathers no foam." And sometimes Uncle Bert would mix and match French and English to get, say: "*Too la monde* likes a cow you can milk through the fence." The world was always feminine to Uncle Bert.

"What does he want now?" said my uncle.

"He says he'll see you again next week," I said.

"That's what I thought he said. Of course. Yes. *Oui. Oui. D'accord. Mais oui. D'accord, à bientôt. Merci. Au revoir. Bon soir. Bonne nuit. Mais oui. D'accord.*" And a final "*Toot Sweet*" as Uncle Bert put his beret back on.

In such conversations my uncle might have used up a good ten percent of his French vocabulary, a vocabulary he doubled and tripled with nods and smiles and gestures and winks, along with the few idioms he knew, often with no regard to the matter at hand. In the end, and taken together, sight and sound, an aphorism here, a cobbled phrase there, plus a *tant pis* French shrug for good measure, my Uncle's poor French was plausible in its way: a *patois* of its own.

What was not plausible was his accent: a cross between the East Texas drawl that was his own and something like a high pitched Cockney—the latter laid on ("slathered" might be a better word: it would be his word) because of my uncle's conviction that French should not only *be* "foreign," but *sound* "foreign": Eliza Doolittle cum Slim Pickens ordering *pommes frites* with chicken fried steak. It was not only less than *loverly*, it made a noise that never failed to produce suppressed mirth from those in our village who heard it. Still, I had the sense then, and I retain it now, that Uncle Bert more or less understood what he was talking about in a language he did not know and could not pronounce. Between the two of us we could get on. In fact we did. *Mais oui.*

Uncle Bert was my father's older brother and to even my young eye and youthful sensibilities, they could not have been more different. My father was trim and tall, and had an ease of elegance about him, both in the way he carried himself and how he dressed and talked. My uncle's belly hung over his beltless britches; his shoes were ripped where a big toe had poked out the front end of the left one, and a calloused heel had split the back of the right one; his hair was wild as John Brown's in the great Curry mural my school class had visited the year before I left for France. And instead of a crisp walk like my father's, Uncle Bert walked like his battered, gray Deux-Chevaux that was full of creaks and rattles with a decided tilt to one side even when it was not turning. My uncle was not yet forty when I lived with him; he seemed sixty. And he affected it.

"I was born to be old," he said to me. "Tell me how to say that in French. Ask your teacher. I'd like to know. I'll memorize it. I've memorized some French sayings since I've been here. Give me age. It is my fate." And then Uncle Bert would wave his hands above his head, palms facing out, in what I came to learn was his all-purpose gesture of exuberance and happiness, something like Anthony Quinn does as Zorba the Greek dancing on a quay. In Uncle Bert's version he'd not only dance with his hands above his head as we'd walk along, he'd wave them out of the top of his Deux-Chevaux when it was warm enough to roll the top back, steering briefly with his knees as we motored ahead. His gesture was so much a sign of him that I'd see villagers greet him with it themselves as he approached; and once I saw two men talking on the street in Lamothe and one of them put both his hands in the air and waved them palms out. The other man nodded, and they both smiled when they saw me, and then they made the sign again.

"And while you're at it, learn how to say 'it is my fate' in French," my uncle said. "I'll memorize that as well. You should hear what French I've put to memory."

Uncle Bert not only wanted to be old, he wanted to be old and French. He wanted to be a Dordogne peasant, not unlike the men we would see driving a donkey cart out of the hills behind our village, or walking ahead of their wives on the long trek down the narrow road to Castillon on market days. He wanted to be one of the men we could see through the open doorways of their farmhouses as they took lunch, tearing their bread with big hands, a liter of wine on the table, cursing the clerics and the Parisians. Uncle Bert would be an old French peasant in a black beret pouring the last of his wine into his soup; a man with his own language, which was neither his nor theirs: "*Il trouve le destin*," if that is what he meant. I never told him. "*Il trouve la morte.*"

Sunday

I live in Paris. I have lived here for twenty years. I work for the English-language magazine *France in English*. We recycle articles about France from other magazines: "Gallic, the oldest wine," "Elizabeth David: The English Writer on French Cookery," "Mauriac château Opens as Museum," "Balzac's Paris." That kind of thing.

Our subscribers are the English and Americans who have settled in France and who don't read much French. Some are here in Paris, but mostly they are in the south of France, Provence and the Dordogne. The Ardèche. The Pyrénées-Orientales. I looked at our subscription list the other day to see if we mailed any issues to Sainte-Foy, Castillon, Villefranche, Lamothe: and we do. I did not recognize any of the names, but then I did not live there long enough to meet many people. Besides, I stayed with my uncle, and through him I met mainly peasants.

We have a back page titled "La Résolution" that is a *récit* about France: sometimes about confusion *à propos* language; other times about farewells, bittersweet or otherwise. I am the writer of "La Résolution," a task that is pleasing for me in an ironic way because while I believe in "*La Fin*," I do not believe in "resolutions,"—either French or English. When I write "La Résolution," I write in order not to reveal myself. In so doing I am not always true to the facts. It is from these duties I am taking the week off.

I have never married. I suppose that a single man, fully and pleasantly employed, with a long lease on a furnished apartment in the 7th Arrondissement, and with a decent palate for *vins fins*, must be in search of a wife. But I am not.

My apartment is a fifth-floor walk-up on Rue de Poitiers not far from the Musée d'Orsay. Another floor up I have a small office. It is where I am now with my tabula rasa and my Olympia Splendid 33 typewriter. My friends say that over the years I have gotten stuffy. No doubt.

From here I have a cubist view of Mansard rooftops and photogenic *rues*. I can see today's bird market on the Quai du Louvre. I can see Montmartre, or rather half of the dome of Sacré-Cœur, rather like a slice of moon in a Chagall. At night the lights from tourist boats that head up and down the Seine blaze through my windows creating a strobe-light-disco-starry night. I am not so high up that I don't hear street noises. And with the windows open, smell the chestnuts roasted by the small old Moroccan man just across the street. It is all pleasant and pleasing in ways that I cannot explain, even to myself. Perhaps especially to myself—if that is what I am doing.

In summer, Paris gets hot and crowded: but I don't much mind. I rather like the city when it is filled with a plethora of Mr. and Mrs. Bridges standing in front of the Grand Palais asking directions to the Grand Palais. In winter, the city is not all that cold compared to Kansas winters, and you can again walk in the smaller streets for decent stretches before a taxi honks you off.

And I like the rain. I like coming into my restaurants and cafés and brasseries to get warm and to be recognized. I think the reason I have never married—or even had more than a series of pleasant affairs (and in recent years only with wives who love their husbands)—is because my affection for Paris is persistent, consuming, and easy. When I am tired of it, I shall be tired of life.

I don't say much about myself to anyone at the magazine. As for my lovers, I let them believe what they like. Sometimes I let them think I am a teacher. Sometimes a film critic. I have an Algerian lover who is convinced I am a famous American baseball player who retired to France on "bonuses." Not that she knows what that means, but she lies in bed while I get dressed to go back to work and says in her English: "What will you do with your bonus this year? Why not take me to La Tour d'Argent for lunch? Why not? With such a handsome bonus as you must get."

When I have visitors from the States, I let them believe I am not fully employed, that way they have something to talk about on their flight back. I have never told my sister exactly what I do; however, I once wrote my mother (after she had been "put away") that I was living in our house in Kansas City where I was employed by an insurance company. I went on to write that I was tending to the privet and keeping the house clean and neat for her return.

I had hoped the letter would give her some comfort (and perhaps it did), but somehow my sister found out (probably from the friend I used to post the letter from Kansas City) and wrote me saying that it was a "terrible and unchristian lie" I had told my mother.

I walk to work, which is in the 15th. And back. My café for weekday evenings is Balzar or Café St. Germain. I take lunch with my colleagues at Le Bistrot d'André with its walls populated by pictures of Deux-Chevaux. I take friends who are visiting from America to la Closerie des Lilas so they can say they've been there, and I show them the statue of Marshall Ney and give them a Xerox of Hemingway's passage about Marshall Ney so that they know where they have been. I meet my lovers at La Marlotte, where we take the side room instead of the front one, even though the front one is thought to be better. My favorite museums are the Delacroix, the Maison de Victor Hugo, and, perhaps predictably, the Musée-Carnavalet. Saturdays, I watch the men play *boules* on Place Dauphine (where I also used to watch Yves Montand watch the men play *boules*). I watch the river from the Pont des Arts. Of course.

When I walk, I look up, only ahead when necessary, seldom at the sidewalk itself. I remember Emma Bovary running her finger along the streets on a map of Paris and wishing she were there—more to get away from Flaubert, I suspect, than from Charles. But as I am the author of myself, every Sunday about one o'clock, I write myself across the Pont Neuf to take a long Italian lunch at Il Delfino. The prosecco is always cold and crisp. The barolo firm. The room one step down.

Thus I turn the pages of my life where every day I read it along a breadth of streets and bridges heading roughly in the direction in which I am going. Always what I have seen before delights me more than what, if I happen to get out of my way, I notice for the first time. It is as if the familiar in Paris is new, and the new is, well: *l'étranger*. Over the years, the city has created in me a curious xenophobia: I wonder what it portends? Will I only reread old novels? Watch only old movies? Look at Uccello and Bonnard endlessly? Attend only concerts where they play Corelli? Rewrite the previous pages of my "Résolution" instead of typing fresh ones? Recreate my old rendezvous with old lovers (will they have me?), instead of making new ones in new cafés? *Tant pis*, as my Uncle Bert might have said (turning the French *pis* into a Texas piss). But maybe not. The streets I revisit still smile on me with the bloom of novelty.

It was to this Paris, to this life of mine, and mine, alone. To this singular and tawny and warm October, to this garret above my apartment, that there came two days ago a letter from my sister telling me that our mother has died.

Monday

Summer was short that first year in the Dordogne. By September and school and *vendange*, the weather was cool enough so that my Uncle was warming the mornings with a kindling fire in the small fireplace at the east end of the apartment. Later, he would light the *butano*—but only in the mornings and evenings. Otherwise "*Le Train Omnibus*," as he called our home, was cold by day and night. There were times from November through March when, if the sun was bright and there was no wind, it was warmer outside the apartment than inside. I remember more than once putting on my coat to go up the stairs after school.

The food of that winter was *soupe éternelle*, complimented on random nights by confits, various patés, and French and Dutch cheeses—all stored along the edges of our windowsills when the weather was cool.

For lunch (I walked home as all the children did), we'd have what Uncle Bert called "*gros croque-monsieur*," the recipe for which (as I once published in La Résolution) is as follows: four or five slices of stale bread slathered with olive oil and mustard, and doused with *herbes de Provence*. Top the bread with thin slices of onion (shallots may be substituted if you've recently traded for them at the market), then thin slices of tomatoes, cuts of *chévre* that is getting more than a little old and thus hard—and thus easy to slice thinly. More *herbes de Provence*. (Notice the absence of ham.) Put under a broiler (the one we had was part of a very dangerous small propane oven that would from time to time burst into flames and cremate whatever was in it, including not a few *gros croque-monsieurs*, and once a *confit de canard* that had come our way) until the cheese melts its way down and around the tomatoes. Serve with cool Montravel Moelleux wine, giving a watered tumbler to any growing Kansas boy who happens to be living with you in your train station. Boy returns to school with a slight buzz about him. Consider it practice for future Paris lunches.

"A *gros croque-monsieur* is made *gros* by slivers of layers and layers of slivers of layers," Uncle Bert would say, as he'd slice his ingredients as thinly as possible. He pronounced the *gros* as *gross*, giving it what he thought was its essential French meaning by drawing it out: *grooooss*; and then he'd pat his belly with the same open palms that he'd wave above his head.

"It's the way I'm made. A sliver of confit, a lump of *pain au chocolat*, a sliver of *paté de duck*. A slice of *pâté d'amande*. *C'est moi*. They have a saying in France: *Never trust a fat man not made of layers because he hasn't lived.* No, he hasn't. Not enough to know you don't feed an ugly pig the staff of life. Or that when the bread is stale, the tomato must be ripe. I am a brioche," he would say, and pat his stomach. Nobody could make *grooooss croque-monsieurs* like my Uncle Bert.

As to our other meals, I remember the cupboards and the window sills of the train station going down to bare over time, and then all of a sudden they were full again. Not with cans and packaged goods as we had in Kansas City, but with small boxes and paper bags and glass jars. Out of these my uncle assembled dinner. Breakfast year-round was *pain au raisin* or *pain au chocolat* or croissants, bought at a discount in the afternoon in the bakery-cum-news stand that is still there—at least the newsstand must still be there because they take our magazine.

Some nights we had boiled black sausages over rice. Sometimes freshly butchered duck or chicken. Once we had foie gras, and along with it my uncle drank a sweet white wine that I suppose was made by one of the peasants with whom he did business. He let me have a sip. With each taste of his foie gras, my uncle would say: "*C'est une petite sotte. C'est une petite sotte.*" By then I had learned enough French to wonder if he had the goose in mind or if it was a toast to someone I never came to know.

Or maybe I did.

Looking back, Uncle Bert must have been some kind of low-grade, black-market trader. I can't remember if I thought that at the time, but I probably did in the way children understand adults for what they are—and then it is settled. Not judged, just settled. In any case, when you are young it is never clear how the adults with whom you live support themselves. And money was not so much in the news those days. I learned later my uncle received a check each month from my father to pay for my expenses, but he never cashed them and it was on that balance—discovered by my Oklahoma grandmother years later—that my sister and I went to college. As for when I was living with him, I always had a few francs in my pocket; I never went without or was hungry. Cold sometimes but not hungry, nor wanting much of anything money could buy. I was privileged in that way. It is my inheritance.

You get used to a different life rather quickly when you are young, at least I did; in fact, my fifth grade Hickory Grove girlfriend and my fifth grade Hickory Grove teacher and my baseball glove aside, living with Uncle Bert in France above a train-station in the middle of wine-and-*confit de canard* country seemed not so much a change as continuation. Baseball gloves and soccer balls are pretty much the same thing to young boys. Young boys and girls are pretty much the same thing to one another.

And I liked my uncle. Not in the same way as I saluted my father. But I liked being with my uncle. I liked helping him with his "work." And unlike my father, my uncle needed help. With each translation I made for him I moved up a notch in my age toward his.

In the mornings between the time I got up and the time I got dressed my uncle would put out the pastries he had bought the previous evening. Before I left for school, there were questions to be answered and a routine to be followed: Had I brushed my teeth? Had my "system" worked? How had I slept? Any bad dreams? He made sure I had my school books. He checked on my lessons. And more than once he visited the school and talked to my teacher who, as luck would have it, spoke better English than my uncle's French. I was doing fine, she said: With her help I would develop a splendid accent in the Parisian style. Wouldn't I like to live in Paris someday, she asked me in French.

"What'd she say," asked my uncle. "I'm bum of hearing."

"If I wanted to live in Paris someday," I said.

"*May we*," said my uncle. "*Tray Bone. Been sewer. May we. Toot sweet.*" My teacher and I smiled. "That way," my uncle said, "he can come to Lamothe and visit me." It was our fate that I never did.

Monday Evening

I have read over what I have written so far in this diary, and in order to be honest with the innocent blank sheets of paper rolling through my Splendid 33, I need to confess that I have not always been true to the facts about some essentials:

My grandmother lived in Texas, not Oklahoma. My mother *did* wave goodbye when I left for New York with my father, but not very directly nor forcefully. I cannot see the bird market on Quai du Louvre, but I know it is there and I imagine it. I did not see Barbra Streisand at La Marlotte as I was going to write when I mentioned the restaurant, but at Balzar shortly after the café was written up in the *Herald Tribune*. I don't much care for Corelli, and therefore would never attend a concert where his music is played. Better Satie. I do like Uccello. I thought about writing a scene where I spoke with Yves Montand, but I did not, and I did not.

There are other details I have also altered in this transcription from life to text. Why I can't confess them just now, I don't know.

Perhaps it is a matter of not wanting to waste honesty on mere facts. Montaigne says: The man who writes while sitting in torn breeches should first mend his breeches. Is this what I am doing? What does a blank sheet of paper know? Out to lunch with a lover. This is true.

Tuesday

Uncle Bert's "business" was with the local markets: Sainte-Foy on Saturdays; Castillon on Mondays; Villefranche on Wednesdays. Others on other days. During the school year my uncle would take me to the Saturday market in Sainte-Foy-la-Grande about twenty kilometers toward Bergerac. Even though it was after the war and many of the markets in our area were impoverished, often with not a dozen eggs, nor more than a chicken or two for sale at this stand or that, the one at Sainte-Foy seemed rich—or at least it seemed so to me. I believe it still exists.

By Friday night, the Deux-Chevaux (out of which my uncle had taken the back seat and put it into the apartment where it served as a couch) would be loaded with brown cardboard boxes of uniform size that I know now had been used as wine cartons by the less expensive châteaux who sold their *vin de pays* to the hotels and restaurants in the area. Each carton had the corners of its top tucked into one another to keep it closed. Sometimes these boxes were heavy; sometimes not so heavy. Sometimes I could hear the sound of bottles clinking. Sometimes I could smell food. At times, there was something alive in them. Often I smelled tobacco and I would as well notice that the peasants with whom my uncle dealt smoked American cigarettes. Sometimes in addition to the wine cartons there were boxes with U.S. military markings on them.

"Don't open them now, son," my uncle would say. "I've got them all tucked down *toot sweet* and packed *tray bone*. Just so."

Usually there were ten to a dozen of these boxes and, on some occasions, a few brown paper bags as well. Whatever was in them, they weighed down the back of the Deux-Chevaux so that the nose of it pointed more up than down. It was as if my uncle had taken to walking like my father: shoulders back, head high.

At Sainte-Foy it was my job to help my uncle carry the cartons to various tables the peasants had set up along the streets, and—as my French improved—to do translating. If a box was too heavy for me and my uncle had to carry it, I'd clear the way—especially if we were late and the streets were already filling up. When we arrived at the appointed table, Uncle Bert would greet—and be greeted by—this man or that man, sometimes waving their hands at him palms out: *Peasants tous.*

"*Ça va! Oui. Ça va. D'accord. Oui. Bon. Tant pis. Oui. Très mal,*" Uncle Bert would say, half Texas cattleman, half a character out of Shaw. (And another half Walter Brennan, now that I think back on it.)

My uncle could spread these exchanges out with nods and shrugs for two to three minutes at the end of which he would first pry back the flaps of the box to see if it was the right one for this particular table and, seeing it was, start up again: "*Beaucoup. Bon. Oui. D'accord. A demain. Après déjeuner. Oui. D'accord. Mais oui.*"

When his business was done (tallies made, accounts settled), my uncle and the peasant would say goodbye by brushing the backs of each others hands in the custom of that country, after which we would return to the Deux-Chevaux to get yet another box; then back to another table to repeat the process. *Mais Oui.*

Sometimes Uncle Bert and the peasant with whom he was dealing would step away from the table; and more than once I'd see money change hands in a fold of old francs: peasant to uncle, uncle to peasant, all of it done while the men faced the wall of whatever building ran behind the table, as if they were—as Uncle Bert put it—"making water." Only "making water" by men in the Dordogne in those days was more public than exchanging money.

Our business was usually over by ten and afterwards my uncle would take a grand crème in the "Orange Café," a small establishment a street east of the main square. From there we could see twenty or so tables and stalls of the market itself: Dutch cheese sold at one; *chèvre* and sheep cheese at another; Pyrenees cheese at yet another. A girl about my age guarded a few cages of rabbits and some live chickens bundled together by twine at their feet. Every once in a while she'd pick up the chickens—usually two or three of them together—and hold them aloft, not speaking a word, but just letting the chickens flap and squawk, as if to show they were alive and healthy. I never saw anybody buy her chickens. She never looked at me. Or at anyone directly. She had tiny, delicate ears, and her ears were the first feature of a woman I remember admiring.

There was also on that street a man with a foot-pedal grindstone who sharpened knives and sickles and shears. I liked the smell of the grinding metal. Another man in a large black beret wove baskets while selling what he had woven the previous week. There was an Englishman who sold mohair scarves and sweaters and socks, and that winter my uncle bought me a pair of black mohair socks to keep my feet warm. I wonder what has become of them. He also bought me a dark red scarf. I know what has become of that.

In other parts of the market were fishmongers and sausage sellers. One man sold oysters. There were families my father would have called truck farmers had they been in Kansas. They had beans and beats; tomatoes and potatoes; turnips and onions. In the late summer they had wild blackberries; in the fall they had mushrooms; and, if you knew the right table and who to ask (and how to ask) you could get truffles. My uncle could get truffles.

From one table you could buy very old Armagnac; from another foie gras. Many of the tables that sold farm produce sold bottles of wine as well; some had labels and dates, others did not. One man sold wine out of a barrel from the back of a cart that he pulled into town with a donkey; you could fill your own bottles or jugs: which is what my uncle did. A very fat woman who always wore the same yellow dress sold huge sunflowers well into the fall. Some Saturdays my uncle would buy a bunch as we walked out of the market.

In those days you could also buy *eau de vie*, a clear *digestif* made from plums or pears, among other fruits. One Saturday the *eau de vie* maker himself arrived towing what looked like a small steam engine behind a tractor. It chugged and puffed, and puffed and chugged, and then finally out of funnels in the bottom came the drippings of the *eau de vie* itself. You could take your bottle, fill it, pay him a few francs and the *eau de vie* was yours. In winter it was my Uncle's favorite drink: my pharmacy, he called it.

"Give me age. It is my fate. Give me my pharmacy to help me with my fate." If he drank more than two glasses he'd either repeat the French sayings he had put to memory, or quote one his botched aphorisms: If he drank more than three glasses he'd look into the bottom of his glass and say something I never understood, in what language I did not know.

Everywhere in Sainte-Foy there were live animals for sale: chickens and quail and ducks and rabbits, along with litters of kittens to be given away, and puppies as well. One man always brought a goat to the market and hung a sign around its neck of how many francs he wanted for the animal. The goat was old, had one horn, and was blind. Week after week there were no buyers, even though in late August the price around the goat's neck went down. Then one winter Saturday the goat was not there, although the peasant was, and because he was a peasant with whom my uncle did business, I often wanted to ask about the goat, but out of some kind of fear that had no name to me then, but does now, I did not. I had named the goat Yogi.

Just as we'd settle into the Orange Café, Uncle Bert would give me a few francs with instructions to buy us four ("*quatre*" he would say, pronouncing the *re*) *Jesuites aux amandes* from a pleasant-faced, black-haired woman whose pastry table was near the church on the main square. We'd have one of these each for ourselves over coffee (yes, I drank coffee), saving the second round of pastry for Sunday morning, a special day at *Le Train Omnibus* in other ways as well.

But every so often, I was instructed to buy five ("say '*sink*,'" my uncle would say, "'*sink*,' just like what you put dishes in.") *Jesuites aux amandes*. When I would do this, the woman selling them by the church would smile shyly, her face would deepen in color, and she would nod and then wrap up an additional pastry. *Sink Jesuites aux amandes* cost no more, I noticed, than four *Jesuites aux amandes*. However, once, when I was sent to buy five pastries, the woman frowned and looked down and would only sell me four—even though there was a full tray of them. My uncle frowned as well when I told him what had happened.

"Oh well," he said. "Tomorrow's another *ah-jur-dwee*." What comes around goes around. Throw your fish upon the water even it floats belly up. *Tant piss*." That Saturday Uncle Bert did not buy sunflowers.

Tuesday Afternoon

I see that while I still have corrections of fact to make, more importantly I must do what we editors call "fleshing out"—as if writing were tucking the blood factory of veins and arteries and muscles and fat in and around the skeleton of life. Such metaphors are why writers like myself distrust editors like myself.

Still, because these sheets of paper are both my only audience and my only subject, I need to make myself and my oeuvre about the same size, if not composed of the same "truth." We three (me, my paper, and myself on my paper) are becoming a *mènage à trois* and we must learn to get along in tight quarters, even if there are moments (whole paragraphs of them) when I realize that the *moi* in our mutual *récit* is more sophisticated than the me who is typing it. But that is another problem. First, more flesh:

Back in Kansas City that summer before my father flew me to New York, neither my sister nor I went to our respective new homes very easily. For my part, when our mother told us our fate, my imagination crashed. At that age you don't fear the unknown. Or at least I didn't. I feared what I knew I would lose. The balsa wood model airplane of my father's Corsair that I was building in the basement. My bubble-gum baseball-card collection. The girl who told my fifth grade teacher she "liked me." My fifth grade teacher who told me. My baseball glove. The game of "catch" my father and I played. All of it vanished to a sheet of blankness while our mother trembled. And then cried. My sister ran to her room: I ran away.

I went out the back door with nothing but an intention of fleeing and hiding. In fact, I got a good deal farther than the Mission, Kansas, Crown drugstore where, in a Norman Rockwell painting, the owner would have treated me to a cherry limeade and driven me home. I went beyond that frame into pastures that still surrounded—at some distance to be sure—the burgeoning suburb where we lived.

A survivalist of sorts I turned out to be. I was two days and one night on the road. I stole some Oh Henry! candy bars and potato chips from the Ben Franklin just down the street from the drugstore. I lifted two warm Cokes from the case sitting next to the Coke machine in the Texaco filling station on Johnson Drive where my father had his oil changed and where, while we'd wait, he'd buy me a cold one for a nickel. I cut across back yards until I hit farmers' fields. I spent the night in an abandoned barn that had, among other things, boxes of old 78 records. I spent the next morning sailing the records out over the barnyard and watching the graceful path of their flight, betting with myself if they would break or not. My mother and a neighbor retrieved me later that day heading west: lighting out for the territories.

Hauled home, I continued my rebellion by not talking. I'd write only notes. No: I didn't care if my father found me not talking. No: I never wanted to talk to anyone ever again: Ever. (I date my use of the colon as a matter of prose style from this period of my life). No: I was not hungry, and I would not eat my peas: Never. No: *Jamais.*

My sister cried. My mother had an attack of "nerves," and for a while she was "confined" and we were taken care of by our Texas grandmother who had arrived a week or so before. My father arrived a week later, probably as quickly as possible after he learned of the crisis. I remember he got there in the evening, after it was assumed I was asleep. He came in, sat down at the foot of my bed, and seeing I was awake, said that everything would be fine in the morning. We'd play a game of catch. We'd finish the model airplane. He had a new one of his new plane. I could tell him all about where I had gone, and he would tell me all about the Panther he was flying. He squeezed my big toe, and I went to sleep. I dreamt of food.

I see there is a wistful quality to all this as I read it over, as if a squirm of nostalgia has been lowered over these events and changed the light in which they are cast. I especially like that scene where I am tossing old records, precursors to Frisbees, out over the farm yard, more of them *not* breaking—as it turned out—than breaking. But the charm of it all was not present when I lived through it, nor was that charm there anytime in my memory of these events before just now. An unavoidable disparity of life, I suppose. There must be many.

Wednesday

Uncle Bert's apartment was intended for the stationmaster, a rail of a man about my uncle's age. However, through some complicated, and no doubt dubious arrangement, my uncle had bartered for the rooms, while the stationmaster had moved himself in with his family just across the highway and down by the river. All this had been accomplished well before I got there; indeed it had probably been done shortly after my uncle had arrived in the south of France. I never really knew. What I did know was the stationmaster and I would sometimes cross paths on school days, he coming to open up the station for the first morning train and me heading for my first class. I would nod; the stationmaster would not. This was our routine. In some way his reticence reminded me of my mother and so one day I asked my uncle about her.

"She's fine," he said, and then after a pause, and after considering me in the fading light of the afternoon, continued: "She's better. She's much better."

"Has she been sick?" I asked. I guess I didn't know if having "nerves" was the same as being sick. I am struck on remembering these events at how shy I was in raising these questions. I was, for example, too shy to ask about my father at all, although he had been writing me, his mail always sporting various military codes and insignias so that each letter seemed to be wearing its own uniform. Perhaps it seemed to me a violation of his final salute and our handshake to inquire after him with anybody but himself. It was our secret bond. My mother was a different matter.

"Yes," said Uncle Bert. "But she is better now. And she will come and see you."

"Come here?" I asked.

"Yes," said my uncle. "But you should write her. Maybe toss in a little of the French you are learning. *Tout de suite. Aujourd'hui.* That kind of thing. *Très bon. Où se trouve. Mais oui. Vin rouge.* I have her address."

"Will my father come?" I asked. Uncle Bert paused before he answered. It was getting time for the early evening train from Libourne to pass through: the one that would not stop at Lamothe, but go on, an express of sorts, to Sainte-Foy.

"*Put tet.*"

"Perhaps?" I had understood from my father that our separation would be firm and long, and would only end when he came back from Korea and I came back from France. It was as if the two of us were going overseas to do our respective duty, and when that was over we'd return to Kansas City and play catch and tell each other the stories of our adventures. The idea that he might come to see me in France seemed wrong: not part of the flight path. My mother might come and see me. But not my father: precisely because he had not told me so. And if you flew the kind of planes my father flew, and wore the kind of hat he wore, and put your thumbs up in the air to say goodbye to your son, you were the kind of father who knew where you were going.

I remember looking carefully at my uncle. I remember it was the first time I had ever "studied" an adult in my life. When you are young you don't quite know what you are looking at when you look into the faces of those a great deal older than yourself. You probably don't even know to look. But look I did, and even now I cannot name who was in my uncle's face. After a moment he turned and stared out the window as if trying to hear the train that was soon to come down the tracks. *Peut-être*, he said, getting it pronounced correctly this time.

Then I heard the train. First, the whistle as it passed the crossing at Rafin, then the train itself. And then, before it got to us, you could feel its movement coming into the apartment from the ground up. There was a red coffee cup and a saucer that my uncle used only on Sundays for coffee with his *Jesuite aux amandes*. The rest of the time he kept it in a shelf with books and letters. When the train crossed the road by the wine cooperative the cup would start rattling in its saucer, and it would not stop until the train passed the far end of Lamothe on its way to Montcaret, St. Antoine, and Sainte-Foy.

As the train passed on this particular evening my uncle turned his head to look at the cup. He waited for the vibrations you could feel in the apartment to stop. He waited for the sound of the train itself to fade down by Montcaret. And when it was again mostly silent, he waited beyond that. And then, speaking less to me than to himself, he said the only complete French sentence I ever heard him utter: "*Nous ne dirons jamais l'essentiel même quand nous en avons la prétention.*" He'd pause between each word so that they were like cards laid out on a table, and while his accent was not improved because of the success of his memorization, his pronunciation was. At the end, he paused again. For a moment I thought he was about to repeat himself as sometimes he would when he'd have a third *eau de vie*, but he did not. Instead he got up and went into our kitchen to light the butane burner and start our dinner.

It would be early in the following summer, arriving by the afternoon local Libourne-to-Sainte-Foy-to-Sarlat train, that my mother would come to see me. She would come to see me about my father. She would not be better. It would be my fate.

Thursday

There was an owl that lived in the attic above the train station, and my uncle said I could name him and so I called him Hooter. Hooter would fly out about sundown and head east down the train tracks toward the cemetery into the darkness. Sometimes in the morning I could hear him return, and once I was looking out the window when I saw Hooter bank up and into the hole that led to the attic.

In the summer and fall—or even in the winter and spring when it was warm enough—my uncle and I would sit on the benches that lined the walls outside of the train station and watch for Hooter to leave. My uncle would measure his one-a-day glass of *eau de vie* against the impending flight of the owl, taking a sip here and then another, until Hooter flew, and then Uncle Bert would tilt off his drink. *La Blanche Dame*, my uncle would say of Hooter. I had learned in school that in French colors went behind the nouns they modified, but even though I was my uncle's translator, for some reason I decided not to be his teacher. Maybe it was our bond. *La Blanche Dame* he would say again just when Hooter could no longer be seen. And then we would go back inside and my uncle would begin dinner.

There was as well some other animal that lived in the train station's attic with Hooter because at night we could hear it running back and forth. To myself I named it Bête Noire because the idiom had struck me as mysterious when I learned it in school. Bête Noire, I remember my teacher saying: it means more than it means. And then she asked me if I understood. *Comprenez-vous? Oui, madame.* I did not.

We also had a cat, a fat white one that my uncle had named Balzac. The families up and down the block just opposite the train station fed Balzac by bringing bones and cheese rinds and other table scraps to a dish we kept just under the roof before you went into the train station itself. Sometimes the stationmaster would bring a mouse that had been caught overnight in a trap set in his office. Balzac would growl and hiss, and while he would eat table scraps from his dish, he would take a dead mouse away. Balzac, my uncle said, was a writer who wore white and had many girlfriends.

In the weeks before Christmas my uncle and I would drive into the hills behind Lamothe and look for the mistletoe that grew in the trees with the idea of making a little money from the English families who spent the holidays in the Dordogne. Mistletoe was also our Christmas gift to his customers at the markets and his friends in the village, and although they accepted it, I later learned they thought mistletoe more a nuisance in the woods than something prized: They were glad the English in Bordeaux and in the near-by villages were pleased to have it. Even pay for it. When I made a gift of an especially fine bunch to my teacher, she at first frowned, then quickly smiled. *Merci.*

"Mistletoe *pour tous les amis du monde*," Uncle Bert would say, taking his hands off the steering wheel of the 2-CV as we went along and waving them, palms out, now inside the car because it was too cold to roll back the roof. "*Les amis du monde.*"

Uncle Bert had a small ladder to climb up to the lower branches of the trees with an army knife and hack off the mistletoe. My job was to hold the ladder. I remember my Uncle saying that what he needed was his Browning Gallery Gun .22 he had left in Texas so he could shoot the mistletoe out of the topmost branches where it had grown into quite large bunches. Maybe when I went back to America I could arrange for his gun to be sent over. It was the kind you could "disassemble" so it might not be difficult to ship.

"*Toot sweet* I'd shoot myself a *grooosse* bunch. *May we*," my Uncle said, aiming his imaginary rifle into the trees and going whap! whap! "That would show them that the best carpenters make the fewest chips. *Mais Oui. Comprenenz-vous*?"

"*D'accord*," I said.

"*D'accord*!" he said. "Well, aren't we learning a little French. Don't tell them back in Kansas you got it from your uncle. I was always the hat rack with a head for only the hat when it came to your mother's family. Whap! Whap! The thief always thinks his pants are up in arms. Or maybe it's that his chapeau is on fire." And here my uncle tapped his beret and plopped the ladder against a tree. "Never feed an ugly pig the staff of life."

In spring, my uncle's scheme for making money was to paint fences and wooden gates with what he called *noir* oil. Black oil was the crankcase oil from trucks and automobiles, and even though the Dordogne was still very frugal from the war and thus most people would do such work themselves, there were enough professional people from Bordeaux and Paris and other cities who had family chateaux in our department to be customers of my uncle. For a doctor from Paris or Lyon he'd change their oil. For a lawyer from Bordeaux or Limoges he'd paint their gate with the oil from the doctor from Paris. I liked the smell of the black oil in the same way I liked the smell of the knife sharpener in Sainte-Foy. It was the smell of something being done. Not exactly madeleines, but each to the smells of our own lost time.

"Best to dig fence posts and *noir* oil fences in the spring," my uncle would say as the two of us would brush away. "That way the ground is soft, and the oil soaks into the wood because its pores are open. And it is better to use hot oil than cold. Right out of the crankcase. Mix it with a little fuel oil and that way it will brush on better. Use everything up in the world, but not *tout suite*, so what comes around has time to go around and drop a few seeds along the way. That's very French. We need a little French in everything we do. That way you get some movement in the monkey."

This latter aphorism (a once-a-day favorite of Uncle Bert's) I use to this day around the office as all-purpose sarcasm when there is yet another slitting of throats in Algeria, a bomb blast in Northern Ireland—or when some religious minded school board in America prohibits the teaching of evolution: There is some movement in the monkey, I'd say, translating my uncle's routine optimism to my routine irony in the flash of an American generation. No doubt it happens in the best of families.

"And don't own anything if you can help it," Uncle Bert would say, usually in front of a large house where we'd be working, or from underneath an expensive car whose oil we were changing. I remember there was not a hint of envy (much less irony) in how he said it. More like breathing than talking. Don't own anything if you can help it. *Dénuement*: A stripping of life to its sensory essentials, if I remember my Gide correctly. I wonder if it leads to *La Résolution*, or keeps us from it.

Thursday Evening

Through my seat's window I could see my father standing on the tarmac while the engines cranked up, and I could see that he could see me as well. He waved. I waved back. As the plane turned, the prop-wash caused my father to lean into the wind and hold his hat, one hand on the top the other on the bill. It was the last time I saw him.

It has been five days since I first typed this. I typed it again just to make sure. Of what?

Friday

A few years ago I received the following letter from one M. Roget of St. Michel de Montaigne, the village in the hills just above where my uncle and I lived. The translation is mine.

"Your grandfather (*sic*) died two days before now and we will bury him as he wished in the cemetery in Lamothe-Montravel. There are matters of his estate that must be settled and you should come to Castillon to do so. His death was natural. If you do not wish to come to Castillon to attend to the matters of the estate, perhaps they can be arranged by an advocate. There is a bank account. There are cartons with your name on them in his Deux-Chevaux which he put there when he knew he was to die and went to the hospital to do so. I hope I have written you at the correct address."

I got the letter about the same time that one of my lovers stopped seeing me, although to this day I don't know why. She simply did not show up at the appointed time at our usual restaurant. I thought of calling her at her office, but decided against it. As far as I know, she was not angry with me, nor had she seen me with another woman (not that she would care). As she was young and had a husband (an American, although she herself was French), perhaps she started a family. Perhaps she was found out—or thought she might be. I used to buy us sunflowers from a vendor just outside the restaurant where we'd meet and then take them back to the apartment where they'd last a few days on their own. The vendor is still there.

After I got the letter from M. Roget, I asked our magazine's lawyer if he would handle my uncle's estate for me. He agreed and also agreed to bring back the boxes from Uncle Bert's car. I asked him not to sell the car, but if it had been willed to me, to make arrangements with someone in Lamothe-Montravel to garage it—and that he has done. I understand it is in a small barn of the farmhouse just east of the cemetery, which itself is just east of the train station. I send a yearly check for its storage and I notice that it is cashed immediately.

This year I got a letter saying there was an offer to buy the car, but I have not responded. In the boxes our lawyer brought back there was dried mistletoe, an American .22 rifle (the kind that can be broken down by unscrewing the barrel), clothes of mine, a red coffee cup, school books, and dishes. There were other items as well. I was going to tell my mistress about the contents of the box the day she did not meet me at the café as planned. No, I was not going to do that. I wonder if she has had a child and it is mine. Our lawyer is a woman, not a man.

On the flight over from New York to Paris, the captain invited me to come into the cockpit, and then the navigator in turn put me up into his dome from which I could see the stars in the sky above us as we flew. I wondered if the stars I saw at home in Kansas were in the same place in the sky as the ones I was now seeing, and I wondered if they would be in the same place when I got to France. Sitting in the navigator's dome I thought I would ask these questions of the navigator or the captain when I climbed down, but then I thought I'd save the question for my father. Nothing in this paragraph is false.

It was just before my mother came to see me that I received the following letter from my father: it was the only one to me that he typed (the capital "B" and the small "r" were broken, while the small "p" would always rise above the line, and now and then there was an extra space between the words, which I took to be the effect of a ship at sea); it was the last letter from him I ever opened.

I have left my father's French just as he wrote it, but on the letter itself I can see my youthful editing: a straight line drawn through my father's mistakes and my corrections printed in a neat, almost typewriter hand, above it. I remember when I did this I pretended that while the letter might have come from my father, it was my uncle's French I was correcting. When you are young you can pretend to yourself in many ways.

Dear *Fils*,

That is French for "son," but no doubt your French is very good by now. Mine is *trés* poor and no one among the officers is any better. We are at *le mar* again and it will not be long before we will make some sorties. In the meantime we are making practice takeoffs and landings. My Panther plane is a very good one, and I have had a picture of me taken standing in front of it for you so you can paint your model to look just like it when we both get back to Kansas City. I will *assistee vous* in that job when I return from my tour of duty. Write your *votre mare* as I think it will do her *tres bonne* to hear from you. She has been *tres mal* since we both left, and when we get back we both must stay put (no running away for you. no war for me) to help her get better. That is love. I will *ecrive* again when I send the picture of me and my plane.

Votre Pere

Saturday Strobe-Light Disco Starry Night

The beauty of Paris is that it becomes more and more of your life as you go along. It is as if, when you no longer want your life to be the sum of the past multiplied by the present, the city slips inside you and you walk on: more Paris than you: Instead of a Kansas Crown drugstore there is a mime dressed as Aphrodite still as a statue, each evening in July, until she earns enough francs for a small trip to Spain. For someone like myself, this kind of Paris is a great advantage. Each day, I shrink and grow. It is a way to live without resolve.

I never saw my uncle again after I left the Dordogne. He must have lived on in his singular fashion with his creaky and tilted Deux-Chevaux and his creaky and tilted French, but I never knew the circumstances. Once, years later, after I had graduated from college and left home for good, he wrote me a letter, a letter that marched through two postal systems and many time zones all the way to Kansas City then back to France to find me here in Paris: in this small room above my apartment. I have never opened it. It sits on a bookshelf a few feet from where I sit. By now it is twenty years old and the flap on the envelope has become unglued and the corners are crumbling. I can see the letter itself, but not the text.

I also have a letter from my father that he wrote aboard his aircraft carrier a few days before he died. It was waiting for me when my mother brought me back to Kansas City. I can tell by its heft there is a picture in it. It too sits on my bookshelf, a row of French books from Stendhal to Gide to Mauriac to Camus to Montaigne to Balzac and my uncle keeping it company.

Have I said (to myself) that part of my college education—and that of my sister's as well—was paid for by my uncle via my father? Have I said that he is the one who, along with the insurance money from my father's death, supported my mother in and out of the "mental" hospital all these years? Have I written about being in the cockpit of the plane and looking at the stars or is that yet to be done? Am I losing track of both the facts and the fiction of my life? I read somewhere that a powerful memory usually goes with weak judgment.

It's not that memory plays tricks on you (as I am sure mine does), but that sometimes it doesn't. You remember all too well. I am at an age where I am beginning to have too much memory. I feel the heft and clutter of it, as if I'm an apartment too full of possessions. My life is stuffed, not with "*objets de luxe,*" but with the less-than-obscure-objects-of-desire from the unaccountable (perhaps "accountable," now that I think of it) acquisitiveness of my mind. I suppose it is the great harvest I myself desired.

And while there are days when I wonder how I got it all up the five flights of the decades of my life, there are more days when I wonder why I bothered. On those days I'd rather have money to count than memories in the brain bank. A treasury bond doesn't have much emotion attached to it, much less extraneous detail—factual or fictional—that has to be rearranged to fit into bookshelves. A Paris apartment with a Midwestern American youth stored in a garret filled with photographs of old airplanes and two baseball gloves, a red mohair scarf, and a red coffee cup is ripe with memento mori. It is only here, one flight up, where I achieve something like *dénuement*—and avoid denouement—as if life were but the last page in a general interest magazine. *Fin.*

Confessions: First: My fascination with the colon was not youthful but recent: I have been reading Dickens: *A murky red and yellow sky, and a rising mist from the Seine, denoted the approach of darkness: It was almost dark when they arrived at the Bank.* Second: "Flowing beer gathers no foam" was not an expression of my uncle's but of Balzac's. Third: There is something my mother is going to say in a few pages that I was planning to claim I did not hear. Fourth: The Moroccan roasting chestnuts below my window is a young woman, and I don't nod to her or wave as I thought of writing when I had cast her as an old man. Fifth: That is not a colon in the Dickens quoted above, although in him they flourish everywhere.

But Yogi, the girl with the chickens and the tiny ears, the woman with the sunflowers, the red cup, the records that I flung out over the Kansas pasture, the letter from my father to me in which I corrected my uncle's French, my Algerian lover, *grooooose croque-monsieurs*, my dead mother, and *tous la monde* there is herein, above and below, and flying out down the tracks at nightfall, or in the attic above: all of it is true, or getting to be true *toot sweet*. Oh, yes it is: Including:

Uncle Bert never said: "We don't talk about the essentials, especially when we pretend to." François Mauriac did, as I learned a few weeks ago when I edited an article for our magazine on the opening of his house as a museum not far from Lamothe. The truth is I could not hear what my uncle said because he had turned away from me as the train was coming through. All these years what I did not know had been said has been a bête noire in my movable attic. To scare it off I have put many different sentences into my uncle's mouth for what I could not hear while the red cup rattled and the train went by. Those sentences, spoken in both English and French over the years, I have sometimes blurted out at curious moments: Once, during a pause in a staff meeting, I found myself saying *I am your father's keeper*. And another time, having fallen asleep in my garret, I woke myself by saying "*Ecrasez l'infâme!*" Also when walking down Rue Dauphine to Sunday lunch I said out loud that *everything would be fine in the morning*. That we'd play a game of catch. And here I tossed an imaginary baseball onto Pont Neuf, all this to, I suspect, the amazement of an American couple heading my way, the man wearing—as coincidence would have it—a t-shirt whose front proclaimed: "Toto . . . I don't think we're in Kansas anymore" down the left hand side, while a silhouette of a small dog barking at a black-stockinged Toulouse-Lautrec dancer was on the right. The woman looked at me with some concern as we passed.

One night, after the last train had gone through, and my uncle thought I had fallen asleep but in fact I was looking out the window of the train station, I saw him walking the rails. It was cold and had been cold and was going to be cold. There was something of a moon, but it was not quite full. There were stars.

At first I did not know what I saw. Then I did. My uncle was balancing himself on the outside rail and walking it west toward Libourne. After a while he was out of sight. Then he came back into view on the inside track, first as something moving in the shadows, then as something stepping on the gleam of the moonlight on the rails. Sometimes both his arms were held out, sometimes not. Once, coming back, when he almost fell, he put the right arm out only and held himself there for a moment, and then started up again, this time coming all the way to the platform without the aid of either arm outstretched. He did not come into the apartment right away, but as he did I could hear that he was talking to himself, but I could not understand what he was saying.

Sunday

When my mother arrived in Lamothe-Montravel she told me my father had "perished" when his plane had been "lost" over North Korea. Then much later that night I awoke to hear my mother and my uncle talking about the "wisdom" of telling me what they had not told my father. They decided it was not "wise" to tell me; however, my uncle thought it would be "wise" for me to stay with him and that he could raise me "*comme le fils.*" That was French for 'like a son,' he explained. My mother said that maybe the matter should be resolved while I was still young. My uncle said firmly, no: That would not be "sage." They would talk to me about going to Kansas City or staying in France in the morning. They would ask me, and maybe they would do what I wanted to do. Maybe not. Above me I could hear Bête Noire running back and forth. Later, Hooter return to the attic. It must have been close to dawn. I also heard other facts of life.

When I was throwing those records and betting with myself as to which ones would break upon hitting the ground, I was also thinking to myself that their flight was like my father's flight: the ones that broke were the enemy planes he shot down.

The ones that did not break were my father landing safely on his carrier. But before I left the barn to get "found" by my mother, I threw one last record and I thought as it left my hand, it is my father's plane no matter what happens to it. I could not stop my imagination: The record sailed as the others had out across the abandoned barn yard, catching this breeze and then that one, so that it twisted first one way then another until finally it stalled, sort of nose up and tail down, before it fell to the ground and did not break.

Late Sunday Evening

From the back-to front-seat where my mother settled me on the train I can see my uncle on the platform. Hooter is sleeping. Balzac has been fed and sits beside his bowl. We are taking the early train from Lamothe to Libourne, then another train to Paris, then flying on to New York and finally to Kansas City, where my sister and I will live as best we can with my mother until I go off to college and my sister takes up religion.

As the train pulls away, my uncle does not wave. He takes off his beret and holds it over his brioche. But he does not wave. He does not put his hands in the air above his head. I don't want to look at him, but I do. It was the last time I saw him.

We All Have Our Stories

The Good Blue Shirt

"I think you give the wrong impression," she said. "And I think you do it on purpose." Irunea was tired of Rob's dinner table stories. In fact, tonight she was tired of all Rob's stories—but it was the one about Tallulah Bankhead that he had told this evening at the Cary's that irritated her the most. And she knew exactly why. None of this "vague uneasiness" that her friend Leslie was always talking about when it came to her husband Turner. U.S. (that was Turner's nickname) had made her "vaguely uneasy" at the Howards' last weekend when he'd brought up a matter of Bill Clinton. Or U.S. was making her "vaguely uneasy" these days just being around the house. There was so much of him. What Irunea didn't like about Rob's stories was that they made him seem self-important. As if he had once known Tallulah Bankhead. Or as if they had once known someone who knew Tallulah Bankhead.

"What impression?" said Rob.

"That we knew her," said Irunea. "And we don't even know anybody who knew her. Ever. I don't know where you got that story. It's the way you tell it."

"Al Tapon told it to us when we were all in Greece," said Rob. He was putting away his ties like he was supposed to, but he was about to hang his good blue dress shirt on a peg instead of using a hanger.

"I don't remember," she said.

"You were sick," Rob said. "I think that was the time you were sick from the shrimp and had to stay in the hotel room.

It was a rough day for you."

"It's the way you tell it," she said.

"How's that?" he said. He had changed into a pair of sweat pants from the athletic team he was on in college, and a t-shirt from a bike trip he and U.S. made across the state every year.

"Well, you never say we didn't know her."

"Why should I?" he said. "I don't say we were there. I just tell the story the way Al did. How could we know her? She's long dead. We're not that old. We've never lived in New York. We don't play bridge."

"It just seems pretentious."

"Darling, you just don't like the 'fuck' in the 'Fuck Betty Crocker' line," Rob said as he went downstairs to watch television. After he was gone, Irunea hung up his shirt properly.

Sentences. Stanza. A Few Lines Even.

Irunea and Leslie were members of a book club that met every month on Sunday afternoons. It had become the rule of the club that each member had to memorize a short section of the book the group was reading and be able to recite it sometime during the gathering. A small paragraph would do. Even a few sentences. If the book were poetry, a stanza was fine. A few lines even, as when Irunea had memorized:

O, learn to read what silent love hath writ:
To hear with eyes belongs to love's fine wit.

The idea to memorize a passage had come from a local author they'd invited one Sunday when they had discussed his novel. He had been able to quote a number of sections from his own work, and at the next meeting Leslie had continued the practice by quoting a sexually explicit description from the Sebastian Faulk novel they had read that month:

"The skin was young and new and almost white, with its patterning of little marks and freckles that he tried to taste with the tip of his tongue." And she went on from there; and everyone knew the passage themselves, if not by heart.

Leslie had an excellent memory and was able to recount quite long passages, sometimes with dialog. But Irunea had difficulty and was always practicing, and even then she'd rarely get it right (she'd recited "...to read what secret love had writ"). Not that the exercise was to be a test of memory, they all agreed. It was just a way of getting into their heads some small part of the book that was important to them, which in turn would lead to a way of talking about the book itself. It was a system of keeping them "on message," as Leslie would say.

Over time, Irunea had decided the best way to get her passage right was to recite it to Leslie sometime before the meeting. Usually, Leslie would stop by Fridays on her way home from work and the two of them would have glass of wine and go over the week behind them. If it was a Friday before Book Club Sunday, that's when Irunea would try out her recitation with Leslie checking her memory against the text.

"*Destroy therefore all your knowing and feeling of every kind of creatures, and...*"

"*Creature,*" says Leslie. "Singular: *creature.*"

"*... creature, and especially of yourself. You're thinking of all other...*"

"*... thinking and feeling...*" says Leslie. "Must not forget *feeling* in this book."

"*... thinking and feeling of all other creatures depends upon your awareness of yourself, for when you have overcome that, all other creatures can easily be forgotten.*"

"*On* for *upon,*" says Leslie, "and you've got it." She hands the book (*The Cloud of Unknowing*) back to Irunea, closes her eyes and recites: "*If you will actively apply yourself to practice this, you will find that when you have forgotten all other creatures and all their words—there will still remain between you and your God a pure awareness and feeling of your own being.*"

"Is that your passage for Sunday?" says Irunea.

"No. It is what follows yours."

"You memorized it just now?"

"Yes."

"How do you do it?"

"I write it out in my head," says Leslie. "I see it being typed in, and it is there. As if on a computer screen. Try it sometime." Irunea said she would.

Ohio Street

Irunea and Rob and U.S. were all in college together. Rob and U.S. had an apartment on Ohio Street and in those days Irunea dated U.S.—not Rob. Rob was dating a girl from high school; Irunea never knew who. Then one Friday night when Irunea was late getting back to the dorm and was locked out because of curfew, she walked down to the apartment. She thought U.S. would not be there because he had told her he was going home for the weekend and not to bother to stop by. But maybe Rob would be there and let her stay, and that way Irunea would not have to "Take A Late" and get another letter from the Resident Assistant. Much later—it was almost morning—U.S. came into the apartment with a girl. But by then Rob and Irunea were in bed together.

When you are young, you do things and don't even think about them. Not in advance, anyway. They don't seem right or wrong at the time, you just do them. When you get older, you do the same, only not as often. It all becomes sections in a story about yourself that you have in your head and that demands to be read now and then even if you don't want to. Like when you had to take a test in college. This is what Irunea had come to believe.

Even after Irunea had *left* U.S. for Rob, she continued to *see* U.S. now and then: *As if they had never finished being lovers; as if there were a natural length to their relationship that had to run its course and unless it did, she would be forever thwarted in her heart, and thus unfinished in her soul.* It was a sentence from a book their club had read sometime ago and that Irunea had memorized, but had not recited to either Leslie or the group. She hadn't felt *unfinished* until she'd read that passage. Still. And why in her mind did she call what she did with U.S. *seeing him.* Even now.

The White House

"And so," says Rob, "the guy sitting next to Sybil Burton doesn't know he's sitting next to Sybil Burton. He's come in late because he's with the White House and those guys are always late to dinner parties. So he doesn't know who he's sitting next to. But his wife does. She's across the table. And of course the whole 'Big Deal' with Richard Burton and Liz Taylor has hit the press. This is when they're filming Cleopatra. So this guy from the White House says: 'Don't we all think Liz is going to get him?' He means Burton. And this guy's wife goes from white to red like stripes on a flag. And everybody at the table doesn't say a thing. Not a thing."

Bike America

"Do you think women talk about sex?" says Rob. "Not think about it. Talk about it." It was late in the day with a bright sun yellow in the west.

"Leslie doesn't," says U.S. "At least not to me. Although . . . " And here he stopped.

"I mean to each other," says Rob. "Like men are supposed to talk about sex in locker rooms."

"Or on bike trips," says U.S.

"Exactly."

One of the rules of Bike America is that you ride single file, and that you do not talk. Even over your shoulders. That way accidents happen. U.S. and Rob should know. They are the co-captains of this year's state ride, and so they were the ones who gave the safety presentations to those who were new to the event. But as they are bringing up the rear of the line of riders, at least they aren't setting a bad example.

"Why do you ask?" says U.S.

"I've been thinking about the difference between men and women," says Rob.

"Why bother?" says U.S.

"Women can't tell stories," says Rob.

"Neither can I," says U.S. "I wish I could. Like you."

"Let's make a list," says Rob.

"Women can't read maps. Women don't remember jokes. Women use more toilet paper. Is that enough?" said U.S. "Women change their mind for no good reason."

"I'm serious," says Rob.

"Why?"

"Because Irunea is all over me about my stories. The one I told the other night about the guy asking Queen Noor's daughter what her father did for a living."

"I thought that was very funny," said U.S. "But the one I like best is the one about Tallulah Bankhead. Standing there in the doorway after all that racket in the kitchen with flour all over her. And those people at the bridge table who thought they were all going out to dinner with her afterwards like they usually did, but no, Tallulah was going to cook instead. I wish to hell I could tell it like you do."

It was the last thing U.S. ever said.

"This Is My Beloved"

The Friday before the Book-Club Sunday (when Rob and U.S. were on their bike trip), Irunea and Leslie decided to have dinner together at Irunea's house. As usual, Leslie stopped by after work and the two of them drank a glass of wine while Irunea practiced her passage, a stanza. She got it right on the first try.

This month's book was by a poet named Lyn Lifshin. The woman who chose it said Lifshin was the most popular poet in America. Irunea didn't much like the poetry, and in fact it had made her realize that for some time now she hadn't much liked anything they'd been reading. Maybe that was her fault.

Irunea had decided she was going to ask Leslie what she thought of Rob telling those stories of his. The ones with famous people in them. Like the one he told at the Showen's house about Queen Noor's daughter. Or the one he told last week when they had all had dinner together so Rob and U. S. could plan their bike trip.

Of course Irunea knew that U.S. and Leslie didn't think that she and Rob knew anybody from the White House, but Rob was going to tell that story all over the place now that he'd told it once. And it embarrassed her. Leslie was standing by the counter that separates the kitchen from the dining room. Irunea was in the kitchen itself fixing a pasta dish.

"We all have our stories," Leslie said. "I tell mine. You just don't tell yours."

Irunea looked out the window for a moment and wondered if that was true. The afternoon had been warm and sunny, and it still was. She was about to say they could eat on the patio when Leslie went on:

"I was always very sexual. I knew it from about the time I was fourteen. I had this boyfriend named Johnny Bullard who kept pawing me front and back, mainly front, and I knew I wasn't supposed to like it and slap his hands, and all those things you were told to do by Miss Taylor, but it felt really good to have his hand on my body even through my clothes, and at night I would put myself to sleep by thinking about what it would be like to be naked with Johnny Bullard and how he'd touch me all over. I even wrote him letters about it, but I never mailed them. I must have used the word 'breast' ten times in twenty-five words. It made me quiver just to write it."

"Who was Miss Taylor?"

"She was the headmistress of Bayonne," said Leslie. "That was the day school where I went. Did you go to boarding school or day school? I forget."

"I went to public school."

"Then my brother came home from college with a copy of *Ulysses*," said Leslie, "and there was a book mark in the back where Molly Bloom talks about everything and ends up saying *yes, yes* all over the place."

"I've never read it," said Irunea.

"Have you read *Lady Chatterly's Lover*?" said Leslie.

"No." Irunea was lying. And she knew the passage Leslie was thinking about. Both the first part of it, and later when the gardener or the stable man—or whoever he was—says something like "it wasn't there for you." Irunea poured them both another glass of wine.

"Well, I did. And I read *Peyton Place* too. And then I read *This Is My Beloved*. And after I read *This Is My Beloved* is when I decided I would take my clothes off for Johnny Bullard and let him look at me and touch me wherever he wanted to. Only by then it wasn't Johnny Bullard, it was Steve Bourg. Do you know *This Is My Beloved*? It's a poem. A long poem. It was thrilling. It was like having tiny words all over your body."

And here Leslie quoted quite a long and explicit passage in such a way that it occurred to Irunea that Leslie might very well have recited that very passage to Steve Bourg. One night? One afternoon? In a car? Down by a river on a blanket? In her bedroom with her parents away for the day? Maybe even to U.S. It was not something Irunea could do.

Then, just as Leslie finished reciting, Irunea remembered again that she did not know the story of how Leslie and U.S. had first met because when asked about it, U.S. would only say they "met in a volcano," which Irunea took as some kind of code between the two of them, and as some kind of signal that neither of them wanted anyone to know anything about.

All of which bothered Irunea, because U.S. knew how she and Rob had met. And now that Irunea imagined that Leslie was reciting a passage from *This Is My Beloved* that she'd once recited to U.S., Irunea said something without thinking:

"Did you know that U.S. and I were lovers? In college. He was my first lover." And then she said other things as well.

Babette's Feast

The only story U.S. ever told was the one about *Babette's Feast* and how he and Leslie had once been invited to a large dinner party that included friends-of-friends so that not everyone knew everybody, but that the foods and wines had been in the movie, which at least most people understood.

The story was that there was this guy there who didn't know about the movie and didn't know very many people at the party and so kept asking to meet Babette. Most everyone thought he was joking, but Leslie didn't think so, so she went up to him and said she was Babette. And this guy was quite impressed and thanked her for inviting him and wondered if she would give him any of the recipes for the dishes they had. He also said it was nice of her to include so many clergy. This was the place in the story where U.S. would say that he had dressed up as one of the clergy, and so had a few other men. Anyway, Leslie says of course, she'll be glad to send this guy some of the recipes, and they exchange addresses, and Leslie sure enough sends him some recipes, but the recipes have some kind of sexual innuendoes to them out of books that Leslie was always reading. And this guy writes back and thanks her, but doesn't say anything about the recipes.

No matter how many times he told it, U.S. would never get the laughs out of it that Rob did when he told it—and Rob and Irunea were not at the party.

The Phone Is Ringing

There are some things you do without thinking, and it is only later that you give them more thought. And when you think about what you have done—what a stupid thing you have said: how you agreed to meet U.S. again, and what forbidden and explicit things you said to him that afternoon, and he to you; how you walked past a woman on the street you knew without greeting her; what a dumb observation you made about politics to the host at a dinner party; how you changed your mind at the last minute about . . . and what a fool you felt yourself to be for having done so; what silly shoes you wore to a reception at the club; or, again, what a stupid and rash thing you said for no good reason   you know (at least at this stage in life you do) that all of these moments will be lying in wait for you when you are in bed at night thinking about what to think about in order to get yourself to sleep.

This is what Irunea had come to believe. And she had come to believe that in very old age, on the very night that she was going to die, every thoughtless and ill-considered thing she had ever done would be there in the pages of her mind as she was trying to imagine better things: the smell of mint; a yellow café in France where she and Rob had once had lunch; the first time she read *Franny*; how, at Ohio Street, U.S. would come up behind her and what he smelled like. And how he touched her that first time.

It was no doubt Leslie on the phone. It had rung insensately twenty minutes after she had walked out, leaving her copy of Sunday's book on the counter. And it had rung again an hour later. And now again, toward midnight. Never mind. Irunea was not going to answer it. Maybe in the morning. For now she would think of the quiet there always was in the house when Rob was gone, a quiet that did not exist even when he was downstairs watching his television where she could not hear it; nor hear him even—except in a vague way—when he came to bed. It was the absence of Rob that would put her to sleep. And it did.

"Who is there?" she said when she heard the door open.

"Me," said Rob. "I have bad news."

Two Conversations That Did Not Take Place at the Reception after the Service

"I just want to say that what I said the other night was not true."

"Then why did you say it?"

"I don't know. I've thought about it, and I can't tell you any reason why I should say such a thing except reasons I might make up that would sound good. But in fact I don't know why I said what I said. None of it was true."

"Thank you for telling me that."

Nor was this said:

"I think you should know something."

"What?" says Rob.

"U.S. and I were lovers in college."

"Not that I didn't know."

"He was my first lover."

"I could have guessed."

"We've kept seeing each other."

Even though Irunea had tried to put herself to sleep two nights in a row by writing into her head what she would say to Leslie and Rob when the time came, as well as what they might say, she did not say anything at all. And now she wished she had not memorized any of it because it meant that the three of them would always be characters in her mind in such a way that she could not write out.

This From the Past

After U.S. had come into the apartment on Ohio Street with another girl and found her with Rob, Irunea would not make love to Rob in the apartment. It didn't seem to make much difference to either Rob or U.S., or even the new girl (who only lasted a few weeks), but it did to Irunea. In fact, it wasn't until Irunea left the dormitory the next semester and got herself a place on Fourteenth Street that she would have anything to do with Rob. Or with U.S. again. But that was later, and this was now. And there were reasons. Bored with Rob? Bored with marriage? A memory of lost time? A way of showing U.S. he had been wrong?

But of course they were not reasons. They were summer blankets and sometimes the cabin of a friend's sailboat. Once a car. Some inflatable tarp one night on an athletic field. Mostly the prop room of the community theater that Leslie was involved with and to which somehow U.S. had gotten the key.

But never at either of their houses, and never at a motel, and not even once in St. Louis when Irunea was there because of her mother and U.S. was there on business, and they both knew it, but did not call one another. Were these her stories? The ones she did not tell.

And there was the last time, just the other day, before U.S. and Rob left for the bike trip, and she had come into the prop room and U.S. was wearing a mask and asked her to name the movie it reminded her of, and she said, *Breakfast at Tiffany's*. And she was right.

Then, sensing him behind her as she had turned away to unhook her bra, having already taken off her blouse, she said: "I don't like this." And that was the end.

Sometimes It Is, Sometimes It Isn't

"Your uncle Conroy writes that he has a fellowship for you," my mother said. I was home on lunch break from lifeguarding at the local pool. "It pays wages and you get college credit. You need good grades in science."

My mother has said this without much enthusiasm. She was reading the letter a second and third time.

Uncle Conroy was my mother's older brother, a pediatric researcher of international fame. In the cultural gulf between our 1950's linoleum-floor kitchen in Merriam, Kansas and Doctor Conroy Watkins directing a medical research lab in Berkeley, California, circa the mid-sixties, there was a pleasing pride—as if in our small house we had a first edition signed by Clarence Day.

"Let me see," my father said. He had closed his auto repair garage for lunch and was also home.

"At the University of California at Berkeley," said my mother handing him the letter.

I have an hour before I have to be on duty at the pool. After closing, I am to take Muff LaRue to Winsteads for a Frosty. My plan is to drive back to the pool for a swim.

"That's what it says," said my father. "A fellowship in Conroy's research lab that could lead to medical school. He should get there as soon as possible for training." My father left the kitchen with the letter in one hand, his meatloaf sandwich in the other, and headed for the front yard to sit in his aluminum lawn chair.

"I don't know that General Science counts," said my mother through the kitchen window.

"Two semesters of *As*," my father said, talking straight ahead.

They were referring to my freshman grades at the state teacher's college of Emporia. I seem to be present only in the third person.

"I'm going to be a doctor," I said to Muff LaRue as I unlocked the gates to the pool.

Muff dove in fully clothed and swam to the deep end. When she got there she pulled herself out and said if I'd turn off the lights she'd skinny dip. I flipped switches.

"I've never dated a doctor," she said. "What kind of doctor?" She walked to the end of the low board, took off her summer shorts and tossed them on the deck. Then she pulled her t-shirt over her head and threw it in the pool.

"A surgeon. I am going to Cal-Berkeley to be a pediatric surgeon."

I was treading water beneath her.

"I'm going to Sarah Lawrence to study classics," she said as she dove in.

I had not been a good enough high school student to go "East" for college. My father had hoped for a scholarship to Yale or Harvard: an Ivy League education was to a young man from Kansas as a wealthy marriage was to a young woman. It went unsaid that the young man present in the third person was thought none-too-bright.

As for my mother, she had discovered that any college in Kansas had to take you if you had graduated from a state high school.

"I think he should stay in our *domain*," she'd say, using in context one of the *ubiquitous* words she was forever trying to teach me.

"He should go East," my father would say without—I would learn later—any sense of history or irony: "Go East," you could hear him say summer evenings in our front yard as he drank a beer in his webbed aluminum lawn chair.

"I think he should stay in our *environs*," my mother would say through the open kitchen window as she cleaned up. That spring I was accepted at Emporia State Teachers College.

"William Allen White's town," my father said.

"Teachers and government workers are never without a job," my mother said.

The summer after my high school graduation, I lifeguarded at the local pool and helped at home: I mowed the lawn, painted the basement walls, cleaned out the attic, ran errands, and hung the laundry on the backyard clothesline. Some days I fixed flats, pumped gas and changed oil at my father's repair garage and filling station. I didn't know what I was going to do with my life, but I didn't sit around looking into a gold fish tank.

At the swimming pool that summer, I saved a boy out of the deep end bottom but never said anything about it until my father saw it as a news item in the local paper. I was the kind of kid who did not explain himself. It seemed natural.

After some discussion, my father won the argument and I accepted my uncle's invitation and went to Berkeley, even if it might have *agitators*—as my father called them, not unlike Dustin Hoffman's landlord in *The Graduate*. On the other hand, my mother feared *impertinence* among the rich students. She told me to find the word in the dictionary she had given me when I left for college with instructions to learn four words a day: *aplomb, domain, environs, impertinence*.

"He'll have to learn some table manners before he goes," said my mother. "At Conroy's they don't 'just eat.'"

It took me a week to quit my job as a lifeguard, say goodbye to Muff, and pack. My uncle met me at the airport.

"So you want to be a doctor?" he said.

"I don't know," I said.

The Billion-Dollar Dream

We were driving over the Bay Bridge toward the East Bay. You have to be a young man from a small town in Kansas to understand how astonishing it is to see the San Francisco Bay for the first time. There is nonchalance about its grandeur.

When I said I didn't know if I wanted to be a doctor to one of the most famous and accomplished physicians in America, a man who had no doubt made special arrangements to get me a fellowship, it sounds, even at this distance, something Californian-sixties: Mellow. Really, man. Yeah. Wow. Far out. That's not what I meant. Perhaps I thought—as we crossed the Bay Bridge to the East Bay—that if I couldn't be a doctor like Uncle Conroy, I didn't want to be a doctor. I'd like to think that now.

"I don't mean . . . " I said as we drove up Grove Avenue past the lab where I would be working.

"I understand," he said. "Don't worry about your future. It is always there."

"Thank you," I said.

From Grove we drove into the Berkeley Hills behind the Claremont Hotel to my aunt and uncle's house overlooking the Bay.

My uncle's laboratory was the Hansen Pediatric Research Center. My first week at work, I had met Hazen: Hazen Edmond Floren Reynald who was pleased to introduce himself by all or part of his name, just as it pleased him to pick one of his names (including his last) and use it for a week. Or this:

"My name is Hazen Edmond Floren Reynald, and you may pick the name you like and call me that from now on. I will remember. But sometimes I won't."

I picked "Hazen." My uncle had picked "Edmond." Aunt Lillian picked "Howard," and no one had told her that was not one of her choices.

"You may change names as I do," Hazen said. "This week I am to myself *Floren*. But you may call me *Edmond*."

Hazen grew up on Russian Hill where he and his mother and Doctor Reed still lived. He was a large-nosed, black-haired, stout-chested, short guy four or five years older than I. He had dropped out of college after his freshman year to travel in Europe: a trust provided him with funds to "poke around the world and among the girls."

"Do you have a girlfriend back in Kansas?" Hazen said.

"Muff LaRue," I said.

"*Rue* means *street* in French," Hazen said. "My mother is French. I understand we are all coming to dinner at your aunt and uncle's house. Very formal. Mother usually brings her favorite hors-d'oeuvres: *paté de canard.*"

I must have looked puzzled because Hazen went on—as if to reassure me.

"Just remember, it is impolite to take the last hors-d'oeuvre, which, if you think about it, means you can't take the second to last piece because you're being impolite to the poor bastard who is stuck with not being able to take the last piece. And if you think about it from here to eternity, you can't take anything off the plate. You just starve."

My mother's fear of *impertinence* had come true.

Beyond our routine duties in nutrition experiments, our "apprenticeship" included working with researchers who had grants to use my uncle's lab. A Doctor Doyle killed hamsters with women's hairspray.

The hamsters were kept in small, square plastic cages designed so you could open and close their air holes. After we sprayed the hamsters we'd close the holes. There were twenty cages, each numbered, and each with a chart that indicated how many seconds of hairspray the hamsters were to get. My job was to run the stopwatch; Hazen did the spraying.

An hour later, we opened the holes to let in fresh air. In the cages where the spraying had gone on for sixty seconds or more, we'd usually find a dead hamster or two. When that happened we'd cut out the lungs and freeze them in small glass containers that had the same numbers as the cages. Doctor Doyle would make tissue slices for study under a microscope.

"What you see is pneumonia," Doctor Doyle said.

Hazen and I took turns peering into the microscope. My uncle was with us.

"Why does it take a grant to prove hairspray is bad for you?" said Hazen. "The stuff is nasty."

"Science," said Uncle Conroy, "is, among other things, the controlled observation of nature that accounts for the variables. Medicine uses science to effect cures. It may be that hairspray is bad for hamsters, but not bad for people. Or that the hamster got pneumonia from other causes. Just because we see the effect doesn't mean we have caused the cause. Or know it."

Doctor Doyle nodded.

"Does your wife use hairspray?" Hazen asked my uncle.

"I won't let her," he said, then peered into the microscope: "Chemical pneumonitis."

"*Hang up medicine,*" said Hazen later in the day.

It was his mantra around the lab: "*Hang up medicine, unless it can prove a Juliet.*"

Living with my aunt and uncle that summer had its pleasures. Even after I moved to an apartment on Derby near the University in the fall, I was always welcome. If they were away (to a medical conference or to a retreat in Mexico in which they owned an interest), I had the run of their house with its splendid view of San Francisco Bay. I was well fed, and when necessary, could use one of their cars. For this, my uncle asked only that I drive Aunt Lillian to the store and on errands.

"Let him drive," my uncle would say. "That way he can learn his way around Berkeley."

When he had me aside he said:

"Lillian is many fine things, but while she can set an excellent table for a dinner party—as you shall see here shortly—she cannot cook a breakfast egg nor drive a car."

"Your uncle thinks I am a poor driver because I am alert," my aunt said one day as we left for errands and to drop me off at the lab. "That is why he wants you to drive. He has told me more than once I am dangerous, but ask him how many tickets I have gotten? None. Or how many accidents I have had that were my fault? None. It is just a prejudice he has about women drivers because we are cautious."

Aunt Lillian had stopped for a green light on Durant because—as she explained amid the honking of horns behind her—men sometimes run red lights.

"You must be defensive in your driving. Defensive and alert. Not alarmed. But alert to what is coming at you from all sides: front, back, right, left. I am perched high and straight in my seat and I am always alert and defensive."

She achieved her "perch" by sitting on a folded pillow so that her head was well above the steering wheel, and not all that far below the car's headliner. From there she could see as well as any present day SUV soccer mom.

"You must be careful of rocks rolling off the mountains," Aunt Lillian said one day when she came to a full stop in the middle of West View Drive, not far from the end of their lane. I looked up the hill at a large rock protruding from underneath a few scrub trees. It had probably been deposited by an ice age.

"Would you like for me to drive?" I said.

"Not at all. You think that rock has been there a long time and will not roll down. That is what Conroy says. But because it has been there a long time means it is more likely to roll down. Hills flatten into plains because rocks roll off them and grind themselves to dust. That is what happened in Kansas. It can happen in California. We have earthquakes. There was a famous one years ago that started a fire. They still talk about it. You must be watchful wherever you are in a car. On the small roads. On the highways. In traffic. In the hills with rocks on them. Just because we are very close to the house doesn't mean an accident can't happen. Most car accidents happen close to home."

"Did she stop at the top of the hill by the rock?" asked my uncle when I told him I had not been able to drive her that day.

"Yes."

I drove Aunt Lillian very little, and I never understood why some days she was pleased to have me do so, but on most days she was insistent that she drive. Nor could I determine why she stopped at some green lights (and ran red ones), but not at others.

"Has Lillian pulled off the road when a truck is coming?" asked my uncle on another occasion.

"No," I said.

"She thinks some trucks are too big for the roads so she'll drive off the shoulder to let them go by. Once I had Triple A pull her out of a ditch, and all she would say was that it was better to be in the ditch than 'squished like a beetle.'"

A few days later Aunt Lillian veered the Cadillac onto a lawn because a cement truck was heading our way, very much on its own side of the road.

"Better up on a lawn than squished like a beetle," she said as we came to a thud of a stop in a well-tended yard. "A wreck involves the police and smashed fenders and a broken windshield and medical bills. Just because your uncle is a doctor doesn't mean we get hospital-care free."

Aunt Lillian looped back onto Stuart just ahead of a woman dashing across the lawn shaking a vacuum cleaner attachment like a fist. At the next green light we made a full stop. At the next red light we drove through.

"Doesn't he look good, Conroy?" said my Aunt Lillian. I was wearing a tuxedo borrowed from my uncle. I had seen myself in a mirror before coming out of my room and thought the same thing: not bad.

"Very good," said my uncle who, I understood, did not put much stock in the formalities of social life but had come to a routine acceptance of it.

Just as Hazen had predicted, my aunt and uncle had invited Hazen and his parents to a formal dinner party. The reason was

Hazen's father's Nobel Prize for experiments (done a number of years before) in which he had taken the amino acid "package" off proteins, then put it back on. At least that is how I understood it at the time.

Aunt Lillian was wearing what my mother would have called "a cocktail dress." Not the kind of dress you saw Harriet Nelson wearing on television in those days (and not the kind my mother owned), but the kind that Olivia de Havilland wore in the movies. It was pale green with tiny gold flecks that seemed to have been woven into the fabric. I had never seen anything like it. Later in the evening, I would notice that her dress matched in a subtle way the dinner plates, goblets, and even a small glass dinner bell that were put out by Bella, my aunt's maid.

"Now use your forks from the outside in," said Aunt Lillian, taking me to the table. "'Outside' being the fork all the way to the left. And do not use the spoon or the fork above the plate until the plate has been changed, and then use the outer one first; in this case that will be the spoon for the sorbet, then the ice-cream cake fork for the ice cream cake that they make at the lovely bakery on Shaddock where they make so many fine things. When you are finished with your courses, put your knife and fork at four o'clock on your plate. That way Bella will know you are finished. And hold your wine glass by the stem, although Howard's mother takes hers by the bowl and puts her—I must say—rather large nose into it. And sniffs quite loudly.

By this time my uncle had escaped to stand in the driveway to wait for his friend.

"Hazen," I said. "His name is Hazen."

I had never been to a formal dinner party, much less in the presence of a Nobel Prize winner. And I had never worn a tuxedo. My brother rented one for the high school prom. My sister's boyfriend picked her up in one for the same dance. I wore a dark suit, went without a date, and stood by the record player and watched Muff LaRue dance to Dean Martin's "Memories Are Made of This."

"When Bella serves a new course," my aunt continued, "it is polite to change the direction of your conversation. You will be sitting between Doctor Reed on your left and Madame de Ferney on your right, and if you have been talking to Doctor Reed for the first course, you then talk to Madame de Ferney during the second course, then back to Doctor Reed for the next course. Madame de Ferney may not converse this way. She has a habit of talking to whomever she wants."

Aunt Lillian paused for a moment and looked at the table, first at one chair, then another, slightly nodding at each, as if more than counting.

"At home we just ate," I said. I thought I should say something by way of thanking Aunt Lillian for telling me how to behave.

"It *is* all a bit fussy," she said. "Conroy doesn't much like it. He says dinner parties are fork-fetish feasts. I suppose he's right, but we women have to keep up standards. Do you see a young lady in Kansas?"

"Muff LaRue," I said, thinking I didn't know the meaning of "fetish."

"When did you last see her?" said my aunt, now circling the table to make some adjustments in napkins and silverware.

"At the swimming pool where I work."

"How nice."

"Yes," I said.

Aunt Lillian stepped back to look the table over at some distance. "Everything is in its place," she said, more to herself than to me. Then: "One more thing. Madame de Ferney always brings the hors-d'oeuvres. A duck pâté on toast points. I will put them on a large plate and we will have them in the living room with some white wine before dinner."

"I know it is not polite to take the last one," I said.

"Yes," said my aunt, and looked pleased. "Madame de Ferney has kept her curious name," Aunt Lillian continued, now looking past the table and around the dining room and into the living room where Bella was putting out napkins and wine glasses on the coffee table, "even though she has been married all these years to Doctor Reed, who as you know, is Howard's father, just as Madame de Ferney is Howard's mother, even though she doesn't have the same last name as Doctor Reed. Or maybe Doctor Reed is Howard's stepfather and Madame de Ferney is his mother. I think that's what Conroy once told me. She came to America when she was very young and brought Howard with her."

"That's what Hazen told me," I said.

"And for some reason I think Howard doesn't have the same last name as either of them because Madame de Ferney named him for an uncle for whom a French village is named. Or maybe she is named for the village. Howard is an only child so I suppose it is easier to do that when you are an only child. And Madame de Ferney always calls Doctor Reed, 'Doctor Reed,' not by his first name as the rest of us do. So we all call her Madame de Ferney and have for so long by now I don't remember her first name, but I think it's Mimi. You should ask Howard. Very curious."

"Hazen," I said. "Howard's name is Hazen."

"Here they are," said my uncle from the doorway.

"There is something else," Aunt Lillian continued, but in a lower voice. "Madame de Ferney keeps both her hands on the table, sometimes even her elbows. She is French. They have peculiar manners. And her English after all these years is still odd. A bit of French mixed in with English. Very odd."

"My mother said I should cut my food with my elbows down, not up. And that I should bring my food to my mouth and not my mouth to my food," I said, again trying to reassure my aunt. But this time she seemed not to hear me and said:

"I am thinking maybe I should seat you ... but no I can't ... that would disturb the arrangement."

"Is it the case," Madame de Ferney said as Bella was clearing the table of the second course, "that in Kansas ... how shall I put it? ... *comment dirais-je? Je ne sais pas ...*"

She said something else in French to her husband. I saw
Hazen frown. I saw Doctor Reed frown. Doctor Reed said
something in French. Then Madame de Ferney said to me:

"Is it 'provincial' in Kansas? Provincial?"

She pronounced her second "provincial" with a certain
prairie flatness, as if to make sure it was not the English but the
American version. Not that it mattered: It was not a word I had
discovered in my mother's dictionary: *Rube. Ff.*

While it was true that Madame de Ferney had used her
forks according to Aunt Lillian's rules, she had not—as my aunt
had predicted—abided by the formalities of conversation; also,
her elbows had been on the table repeatedly, and (my mother
would have been shocked) Madame de Ferney had removed
her bread from the bread-and-butter-plate and put it on the
tablecloth where it left crumbs. And she not only stuck her nose
into the wine glass, she swirled it around before holding it to
the light and said: It is the first duty of a wine to be red.

"Don't you agree?" said Madame de Ferney to my Aunt.

"Yes indeed."

"And from what you call the *environs*. Is that the right
word Floren?"

"Yes," I said. Everybody looked at me for a moment and
then Madame de Ferney asked me what kind of wine we drank
in Kansas.

"My mother has a glass of Mogen David as she fixes dinner," I
said. "My father drinks Coors. My mother is Polish. My father Irish."
In the small silence that followed, everyone took a sip of wine.

"I ask about Kansas being provincial," Madame de Ferney said,
"because I am told they were provincial *ici* in San Francisco before
the *gros* earth cake. The *gros* earth cake and the fire did them a
great good in that regard because the rebel lost their shanties."

"*Rabble*, Mother," said Hazen.

Madame de Ferney paused only to mouth the word *rabble*
silently with what seemed to me impatience toward the
English language.

"Mother's '*gros*' is French for 'large,'" Hazen said to me. "The Great Earthquake."

"Thank you," I said. And as if to show I was going to learn French I repeated "*gros*" out loud.

"You'll need to work on your *r*," Hazen said. I had no idea what he meant.

At this point Bella came to serve another course, while Madame de Ferney continued:

"The families whose furniture came 'around the Horn' began to *assende* and that gave the city its culture. Some people who first arrived in San Francisco brought their furniture with them over the prairie ground in wagons. It must have been very hard on chairs. Not to mention desks and tables. All of Doctor Reed's family furniture came 'around the Horn.' Our chairs are very solid. *Trés solide*."

Madame de Ferney had been speaking to the table at large, but then she again turned to me:

"They have no earth cakes in Kansas to make matters better. *C'est trés mal* in that regards, don't we all think so? Maybe a dust storm or a prairie bison fire could do the same thing. Does your family have the particle?"

"'Quakes,' mother," said Hazen. This time Madame de Ferney did not mouth the word.

"They have tornadoes," said my aunt. "Tell Madame de Reed about the tornadoes. How Dorothy went to see Mr. Oz on the Yellow Brick Road. That might be just as good as earthquakes."

"'Madame de Ferney,'" my uncle said, but Aunt Lillian seemed not to notice.

I was about to ask "a particle of what?" thinking Madame de Ferney might have wondered if we owned a bit of farm ground when Doctor Reed coughed rather loudly a number of times to my left and we all looked his way. My uncle patted him on the back and asked if he was all right?

"I was telling our nephew the other day," Aunt Lillian said when Doctor Reed's coughing spell stopped, "about that big rock at the top of the road, and how it might fall down if we had another earthquake like the one Madame de Ferney has mentioned." My aunt stopped for a moment and seemed befuddled.

"You were about to say something about the rock, Lillian," said Doctor Reed.

"Yes! Well, if it rolled down the hill it would squish that nice bakery on Shaddock where we got the dessert for tonight."

"Ah *oui!*" said Madame de Ferney. "It is a lovely bakery and Doctor Reed always buys something from it whenever we are coming to the University. There is *rien* like it even in San Francisco."

"'*Rien*' means 'nothing,'" said Hazen. I nodded. "'Rien,'" I said, this time doing no better with my "*r*" judging by Hazen's look.

"*Nada*," in Spanish, said Doctor Reed.

"*Nada*," I said, thinking at least there wasn't an *r*. Again a moment of silence while everyone took another sip of wine and Bella bustled.

"And they probably don't have a bakery in Kansas like the one on Shaddock that we all like so much," said Aunt Lillian. "Just like they don't have hills down from which rocks might fall because they already have fallen down and that's why it is flat. And maybe that is why Madame de Ferney has asked about it being provincial. No quakes. No hills. No rocks. No bakery."

"Ah *oui*," said Madame de Ferney, at which point Aunt Lillian rang the bell for Bella who was standing beside her.

"Maybe I should not have asked about Kansas being provincial," said Madame de Ferney. "It is of no matter, but sometimes those of us who live *la vie de chateau* cannot imagine remote places in the United States as being other than provincial. That is true in France as well. We have peasants in many places south of Paris. Some of them harversting their own *poulet*."

"*Chicken*, Mother," said Hazen.

"I know it is 'chicken' in English," said Madame de Ferney. "But I prefer the French. Who can like a word like 'chicken' instead of '*poulet*'? Or 'duck' instead of '*canard*'?"

"It is what we had this evening," said Aunt Lillian. "A recipe right from France. Chicken cordon bleu. Not that we raise chickens or ducks here in Berkeley. I expect there is some kind of rule against it. I know there is one about hanging your clothes out to dry, isn't there Conroy?"

"There is indeed. It is called a 'covenant,'" my uncle said to Doctor Reed who smiled. "As if good taste were a religion. No rabbits in cages. No chickens. Or ducks. No horses or goats. It was quite a list they gave us when we moved here. No clothesline, as Lillian says."

"In Kansas we have a clothesline," I said. "I do the hanging out when I am home." Uncle Conroy looked at me and smiled. I was about to say the Simms down the road had both chickens and ducks as well as pigs they fed, when Madame de Ferney continued.

"It is our own limitation, I suspect, and I would be pleased to learn otherwise. How did your parents' furniture come to Kansas?"

"Here is dessert!" Aunt Lillian said, and once again rang the bell, even though Bella had returned to the table.

The arrival of dessert and the clatter of plates and forks and the general talk about the bakery on Shaddock changed the course of the conversation—or rather the monologue by Madame de Ferney—and as we ate she turned to Hazen and asked:

"Do you remember when you were an *adultlesson* and we took you to Paris?"

"*Adolescent*, Mother," said Hazen. "It is the same in French."

"Yes, I suppose it is," said Madame de Ferney. "It is just that we were showing you where I was reared—is that the word? You raise something like cows but rear children. Do I have that right?"

"Yes," said Doctor Reed. "Edmond was in fact born in Paris but they soon moved to America and he was reared here."

"Conroy and I have not reared any children," said Aunt Lillian. "This is our nephew," nodding toward me. Aunt Lillian seemed either to have forgotten my name or was continuing my family's tradition.

"Ah *oui*," said Madame de Ferney to Aunt Lillian.

"Ah *oui*," said Aunt Lillian. "But do tell us about your rearing in Paris."

"We lived in the Sixth, but below Saint Germain. The Sixth goes all the way to Boulevard Montparnasse, but my father would not admit that. For him it only went as far as Saint Germain. So I was reared in that domain. Is that the right word?" Madame de Ferney asked me.

"Ah *oui*," I said. I saw Hazen smile. "Or you could say 'environs,'" I said. Madame de Ferney seemed pleased at this information and this time said *environs* out loud with a peculiar guttural sound on the *r*.

"My father was *trés* formal and would not even '*tu*' my mother. Of course, he did not '*tu*' me or my sister." Madame de Ferney paused for quite awhile and looked away from the table. The only sound was Bella putting out coffee cups in the living room.

While Madame de Ferney was thinking of her days growing up in Paris, for my part between the rocks tumbling down and squishing the Shaddock bakery, the tornadoes that might be as good as earth cakes, covenants against chickens and clothes on the line, I had been thinking in bits and pieces about home: my father's webbed aluminum lawn chair and how he took my uncle's letter and his meatloaf sandwich outside and read the letter while my mother cleaned the kitchen counter where we "just ate" on summer nights, my mother having her glass of Mogen David wine while she cooked with no idea about its duty, my father with his beer in a bottle after dinner as he read the paper or, on Fridays, watched boxing on television.

And it wasn't when Aunt Lillian asked me about a girlfriend that I had thought of Muff LaRue. It was when Madame Ferney was talking about chicken *poulet* and duck and *canard*. How, after both Muff and I got dressed and, not having gone "all the way," sat in two chairs under my lifeguard stand and talked into the night about our futures: me to California to become a doctor, she going East to Sarah Lawrence to major in classics—and I thought then that studying classics at a fancy East Coast college for girls and skinny-dipping in a Kansas municipal pool with the lifeguard somehow didn't go together. But I did not say so.

Later I drove Muff home, and we promised we'd meet again over Christmas break—at the swimming pool, cold and snow or not. Assuming my key still worked.

My aunt fingered the spoon on the top of her plate. She picked up her wine glass by the stem and studied the color. She rang for Bella.

"Thank you," my uncle said to Bella as she began clearing the table of dessert plates, all forks now at four o'clock.

"*Maintenant* that you are *ici* in Berkeley," said Madame de Ferney, "do you think it provincial in Kansas?"

My uncle was about to speak and so were Hazen and Doctor Reed when I said to Madame de Ferney—and, with considerable *aplomb*—to the rest of the table:

"Sometimes it is, and sometimes it isn't."

"Ah *oui!*" said Aunt Lillian

"My mother was blown away by your quip extraordinaire," Hazen said the next day in the lab. "You are quoted on Russian Hill. She thought you were serious."

"I was."

"Did you miss Kansas?" Muff says to me. We are sitting in my father's lawn chairs that I have taken to the pool and put beneath my old lifeguard stand. It is snowing. The pool has been drained, but not to the bottom. There is a skim of ice on what water remains. "I did not," says Muff before I can answer.

"I did."

"Are you going back?" she says. "To Berkeley to be a doctor?"

"Hang up medicine," I say. "Unless it can create a Juliet."

She seems not to hear me and says, "I learned that Socrates took up dancing in old age. So I've started dancing. Modern dancing." She gets out of her chair and does a small pirouette in the snow in front of me.

"I've never dated a dancer," I say.

And then there is a silence between us. I take a sideways glance at her. She is looking at the space just in front of us where she has done her pirouette. The snow is falling faster now and it is filling her footprints. I never knew her well enough to guess what she might be thinking. But I was thinking I would not see much of her ever again, and I would be right about that.

"You haven't said if you are going back."

"In Berkeley," I say, "you don't just eat, and you can't hang your laundry on the line." She gets up from her chair and does a second pirouette, this time putting her toes into the same place where they had been before, and in so doing her feet make their marks in the same place where the snow had almost filled in her previous pirouette. And in coming back to her chair she steps into the same footprints she had made before, and smiles at being able to do so.

As I drove her home, Muff asked me if it were true I had once saved a boy from the deep end.

"Yes."

And it was at the door of her house that she told me it was from Shakespeare ("Hang up Philosophy"—not medicine) that Hazen had gotten his *mantra*, and even used the word, which I did not know until I came home that night and looked it up in my mother's dictionary.

By The Light of the Silvery Moon

I cook at the Corner Pocket evenings when they need me. Burgers. Fries. Catfish. Chicken-fried steaks. Frozen hash browns I toss on the grill. Ribeyes. After closing, I dig graves. We're on the edge of a big time zone so in summer there's light in the west when I start. I watch the sun rise when I'm done. It's a pleasure.

My day job is what I pick up in repairs. Roofs after a hailstorm. Cement work. I've got my own mixer. Sidewalks. Plumbing. Most of us out here are dead or dying so I've got widows who need a leak stopped. While I'm there, could I fix the third step on the way to the basement? Sure. And the screen door needs to be re-hung since the grandkids went back to Denver. Sure. But best I like my graves. I dig them by hand. Not like Harper. Harper uses a backhoe.

Clara waitresses at the Corner Pocket. Not always when I do, but sometimes. She's younger than me by more than I told her. She's tall. I'm taller a bit. She's one of the tallest women we got in and around Blaze, Bly, and Cottonwood. Mostly in her legs. But being tall is not what I like about her. It's her shoulders. The way they connect to her neck. And her face. Open like a charm. Black hair with long curls that hang down her cheeks and spring-bounce when she walks. Also tattooed words on her hands and arms and legs. She says she's part Cheyenne. Could be. Dull Knife's tribe went through White Woman County and left their breed in the settler's wives. I've got the blood, tall as I am.

I'm good at everything I do but living by myself. My lane's junk. Iceboxes from remodeling jobs that I was supposed to haul to the dump. Stoves. Washing machines. Tires. ACs I took the copper out of when the price was high. Trash bags of beer cans the time I started to pick myself up. OSB board that's got wet. Five Roper motel gas ranges from when they did over Pleasant Valley Manor. Maple cutting boards from the same job. Tubs. A couple of couches. A fold out to sleep on nights by the edge of my garden summers. Or sit on with a Dos Equis afternoons. There's a story to the fold out. Two oak pews. My front porch has a pile of plaster that fell off the ceiling that blocks the door. Tilly and I go around back. Tilly's my dog.

Harper says I'm scum. He should talk. His pickup's still in my yard. He ran over a tree stump half way too drunk one night and put a hole in his oil pan. That was three years ago. There's a vitamin-M plant growing in the bed for all the dirt that's been blowing in. More than one. Beer cans. A work coat. Two coolers. Tools turned to rust by now. Other shit. Harper and I go back. But something changed. He won't come down. Not even to tow his truck for parts. Bought himself a new one. Turbo diesel.

I've got six pence, jolly, jolly, jolly six pence. It's a song Clara sings. There are others. I don't have a memory for songs, but she does. Something about having *six pence to last me all my life.* She wants us to sing it *ensemble.* That's one of her words. She says she'll sing some parts and I'll sing others, and some we'll sing together. I can't sing for shit.

I mark my graves with a chalk roller I got from the high school when they dropped the baseball team. Plus two bags of dust the coach said I might as well take. They're in the house. When it gets cold and the wood stove in the basement goes out, Tilly sleeps on them. Talk about your ugly dog. Homemade sin ugly. Bares her teeth like she'll bite your balls off for standing still. But she won't. Bark. She'll bark. And kick the shit out of other dogs. She can turn around in her skin she's so quick. When she's happy she chews tires. Wheelbarrow tires. Rotor tiller tires. The tires on Harper's pickup. They're all flat by now. When I come home she starts chewing my tires before I stop rolling . . . *rolling, rolling, rolling home.* There's a bit more of it.

At the Corner Pocket we get our catfish from a dealer. They're farmed and frozen. I catch mine out of the White Woman and keep them in a stock tank to get the mud out of them. A fish is the water it's been living in. Sometimes I clean one and take it to work for after we close. That's how I start with Clara. I'm cooking my fish on the grill with butter and onions and sliced new potatoes from my garden. It's summer.

What's that? she says. My own catfish, I said. Out of the White Woman? she says. Yes, I said. I know some places, she says. So do I, I said. There's enough to share, I go on. I got McCormick's in my truck, she says. Vodka. We got a plan, I said.

I got two pence to spend, two pence to lend . . . I can't remember it all, but maybe I will. Sometimes it takes time to remember everything. Clara also sings about a skylark. *Skylark, have you anything to say?* She sings it more to herself than me. You go someplace to find the skylark. Or maybe it goes someplace for you and then flies back with a story about where it's been. She sings it some, then stops. Then starts up again. It's a pleasure to hear her.

The last person in my house was Harper the night he runs over the tree stump. We drink a case of Dos Equis and he crashes on the couch. There are two weeks of dishes in the sink with hundred-legs living in them. Clothes on the floor. Dishes on the floor. Beer bottles. Cigarettes in the ones Harper uses as ashtrays. Coffee cups where I've left them. You don't notice your shit when you're going through a case of Dos Equis.

You're scum, Harper says when he wakes up. *Scum* is Spanish for fucked up. You'll get brown recluses if you leave your clothes on the floor. A hole to the bone in your foot is a sure sign of scum. Get fucked, I said. I'm working on it, he says. For sure you won't. What woman's going to like this? Get your shit together and take it to the dump.

That's what he says to me these days. You got your shit together? Or are you still living in it? He thinks I'm trash. I think he's trash for thinking so. But he's right about the brown recluse. Only it isn't my foot but the palm of my left hand with a hole all the way to a bone before I go to the clinic.

I'm married, Clara says, the night we're eating my catfish and drinking her vodka. I didn't know that, I said. He's not around, she says. Where? I said. Minnesota, she says. We just never split the sheets for the judge. Tall? I asked. Like you, she says. I'm not married, I said. I know, she says. More? she says, tapping the McCormick's. Sure, I said.

We drink it iced at the table by the front door like we are customers, only it's just us and the pool tables, and the glow of the Corner Pocket sign in neon outside coming through the curtains.

I made these, Clara says, pulling the curtain to look into Blaze where there's nobody. Sewing's my day job. Digging graves is mine, I said. I heard that, she says. Only I do it nights, I said. I heard that, she says. *Star light, star bright*, she goes. *First star I see tonight*, I answered. She smiles. I could mend that shirt for you, she says. Thanks, I said. We go quiet. Do you know you've got real green eyes? I said. Yes, she says. She smiles again, and this time it's as deep as it is wide. I'm thinking she likes me.

I dig my graves four by eight. I got a plywood frame for the chalk lines. I have a metal one for winter so I can cook the ground before I dig. I do my marking in the afternoons. When I'm done, I cut off the sod and stack it in strips to one side. Then I sit on my tailgate and have Dos Equis Amber. That's not much work to take a break, but I like to look at the other graves to see if I've got mine lined up. It's like wanting things straight when you work carpentry. Even a widow woman who's going to get parked in Pleasant Valley Manor by her Denver kids gets to have her closet square to the rest of the house. And her grave square to her husband's.

When my Dos Equis Amber is a dead soldier, I go home and feed Tilly. Then up to the Corner Pocket if they need me. If not, I work my garden. Sometimes I'll go down to the White Woman and pull a flat head or two. That's what I do the time I share with Clara, only I get a fresh one from the stock tank. Lucky it's big. There's only skin and bones when we finish. No potatoes. For a girl she eats like a horse.

I'm not much with women. I had one once. Maggie. She'd come over and keep the place picked up. She started inside and worked her way into the yard. It was spring and she planted a garden. It was how I got to gardening. She's the one who gave me Tilly. Also the fold out. I liked it. I'll admit that. I liked coming home knowing that Maggie was going to have supper for me and a six pack of cold Dos Equis Amber while we sat on the fold out by the garden. And later we'd unfurl the couch and sleep on it. That was her word. *Unfurl.* I liked it.

You think we should get married? she said one night. It was summer and she'd been waiting on the fold out for me to come back from a grave. I don't think so, I said. Why not? Why? I said. I want to be married, she said. Then find somebody who wants to marry you, I said. How come you won't let me dig graves with you? she said. I could help. Don't you love me? I don't think so, I said.

She pulled on her jeans and left. Came back once to check the garden. Say goodbye to Tilly. Pick up things. I'd see her around Blaze, then gone. Maybe a year ago in Cottonwood I saw her. We didn't talk. Maybe she didn't see me. I think she did. I saw her once or twice with Clara. Harper told me they're related.

If I know whose grave I'm digging, I talk to them. Back and forth. Too bad your liver gave out, I say to Al Johnson. I had fun while it lasted, he says. At least you know I'm digging your hole and not Harper with his backhoe, I say. Make it square to Bella's, Al says. But don't let her fall out on me. I want some peace and quiet as long as I'm dead. Not to worry, I say. Thanks.

Until I met Clara, I worked alone. Then I liked digging graves with her while Willie Nelson's on the tape deck in my truck and her singing along. *If you've got the money, honey, I've got the time.* Or her singing by herself and trying to teach me how to remember the words and carry the tune. I like how we share her McCormick's and not get so drunk we don't talk. You got to like a woman who likes to talk. And not about the grocery-store magazines. Or Jesus. Or television. I got a lot of shit in my house but I don't have a television. I did. Harper threw a Dos Equis through it. When I turned it on it exploded. Glass and wires and white dust everywhere. Not really, but that's what I tell people. Mainly it just smoked and blew a fuse. Better it exploded for the telling of it.

I've been thinking about Harper calling me scum. How you getting home? I said. Lend me your Harley, he says. Sure, I said. After he leaves, I go back to bed. When I get up, I wash my sheets and the clothes off the floor. Five loads. I wash the dishes. Kill the hundred-legs with a spatula. Take down the plastic from winter on the windows. With the new light coming in, I clean up. Toss the beer bottles in boxes. Wash more dishes. Look for brown recluses until I find one. Sweep the floor into a scoop shovel. Then I pick up beer cans in the lane and put them in plastic trash bags. Change the sheets on the fold out. It's coming summer, so I start sleeping out at night. Only I don't *unfurl* it. Just sleep on it like a couch.

Two weeks I clean off and on. Weed the garden. Pull onions and radishes and take them to the Corner Pocket to give away. Put cages around my tomatoes and plastic around the bottoms against the wind we get out here just like Maggie did. Then one day I stop.

Maybe if I'd taken the beer cans to the metal man in Cottonwood I'd keep going. But one night I'm sleeping by my garden and I wake up because Tilly's running a fox and I test myself by starlight to see if I feel any different from when my house was full of shit, and I don't. Then I ask myself if I feel like scum, and I don't. So the house fills up with shit again and I still don't feel like scum. I don't feel one way or another about living in shit. If you don't like who you are, call Doctors Smith and Wesson. Who wants to live with someone they don't like?

That first night at the Corner Pocket Clara talks about words. The words tattooed on her body. On the back of her left hand has Cynic. It's not some guy who doesn't want to vote because politics are shit, she says when she sees I'm looking at it. Or a woman who's had it with men. It's old philosophers who thought you've got to raise your own food. Don't have both a truck for your day job and a car for town like they do in the Rest of America. Don't own anything you don't need, she says.

I didn't know that, I said. Catch your own catfish, she says and taps her fork on the plate. The potatoes and the rest of it are from my garden, I said. She smiles. I read about Cynics at this house where I did their slipcovers, she says. I read, do you? Not much, I said. But I'll give it a try. I have this book, she says. *Cowboys Are My Weakness.* I'll read it, I said. You know any good words? she says. *Unfurl,* I said. Like a flag, she says. Or a fold-out couch, I said. She smiles. I love words, she says. The best ones never leave you. Know what these are called? she says as she pulls one of the curls that hang down along her cheek. *Tendrils,* she says before I can take a guess. Don't you like it? she says. *Tendrils.* It's why I grew them. For the word.

Somebody outside goes by and their headlights come through Clara's curtains. You want to dig a grave with me sometime? I said. Sure, she says. You'll see the sun come up, I said. Fine by me, she says. Yet tonight? I said. Sure, she says.

We finish my catfish and not all her McCormick's to take in my truck. That's when she starts singing *I've got six pence, jolly, jolly six pence, I've got six pence to last me all my life. Two pence to spend, two pence to lend, and no pence to send home to my wife, poor wife.* Thinking about her, I remember more of it. Funny what will crank up memory. For me it's what's in my mind already.

Harper's the one who gets me started with graves. Baker Johnson's casket busts out from the grave next to the one Harper is digging and breaks his great toe. That's what he calls it. His *great toe.*

I'm yelling What-the-Fuck for my Great Toe, Harper says, and the casket lid pops open and there's Baker, nothing but bones and dust and rags and teeth. No thank you, I say. No fucking thank you. I'll dig graves with a backhoe or not at all. That's when he comes up to Corner Pocket and asks me to finish the job. Sure, I said. You got to do it tonight, he says. Sure, I said.

I dig the grave another three feet deep, close Baker Johnson's lid and slide him on down, fill and patch the hole on the side, then tamp everything firm. The next day they plant Doug Johnson on top of Baker Johnson and nobody knows the difference. I think they're cousins anyway. Along with Al Johnson who I bury two doors down. After that I'm on my own. Hand-dug graves for half the price of Harper's backhoe.

Cynic was my first tattoo, Clara says. She's up above the hole sitting on my tailgate. I'm in pretty deep by now. The ground is soft because I haul water to it the first part of the week. Duluth, 1997, she says. I picked it because I liked the way it looked. With the "c" at the start and then the "y" and then just before the "c" at the end there was this "i." It was later I found out what it means. Hand me my level, I said. Sure, she says. The square, too. Here, she says.

It's good work. Even after the McCormick's it's good work. I look up but she's gone to the truck. I hear the tailgate creak. I think she'll be beautiful when I climb out. *Skylark, have you anything to say*, she sings. Help me up, I said, not needing a hand but wanting hers. Here, she says coming back to the edge of the grave with her hand and a smile I can see in the light of sunrise coming.

And sometimes "y," I said as we sit on the tailgate and she offers me the last pull of her McCormick's.

What? she says. And sometimes "y," I said. Like we learned in school. That "y" can be a vowel if it wants to be. In your *cynic*.

I wish I'd thought of that, she says. Then I'd have *c y n y c* that would spell itself in reverse like *kayak* and *radar*. I'd like to have *Egypt* because of those tails that go below the line but I've used my "e" for *ensemble*. What about *radar*? I said. I'm saving my "R," she says. I want to say something, but I don't.

Harper keeps telling me I must be depressed to live in shit. It's something he learned from television. Harper watches television. And listens to talk radio. That's where he gets his shit. His shit is in his head. At least mine is on the floor. And in the yard. You got to know what kind of shit you want in your life because everybody's got it someplace. I like mine where it is.

When I'm frying catfish at the Corner Pocket or working my garden or digging graves with Clara, I'm happy. How not to be happy with a tall girl younger than yourself who likes spending the night drinking McCormick's in a graveyard and talking about the words on her body? And who can't like an ugly dog that's so happy to see you she chews tires?

No cares have I to grieve me, no pretty little girls to deceive me, I'm as happy as a lark, believe me, as I go rolling, rolling home. There you go. That's more of it. How not to be happy when you can remember a song even if you can't sing for shit?

The graveyard at Rose Hill has the best view. It's the township cemetery. If you're a Christian, you don't want to be buried there because you'll be in the ground with Seculars. That's what Pastor Black calls them. Seculars. I've dug graves for his dead as well as Father Wilcox's dead. Dead's dead, I think, no matter whose graveyard you're in. But Rose Hill's the only place I take Clara. It's where we watch the sun come up that first night. And the moon go down. *By the light of the silvery moon.*

From Rose Hill you can look down the road that curves into Bly and the grain train tracks that run by the Co-Op where The Committee to Save the World meets. We don't really save the world, but some days we talk like we can. Ranchers. Wheat farmers. We trade jokes. The same ones more than once. Ones you can't tell in the Rest of America. You'd think in a free country you'd be free to tell jokes. Maybe that's their shit, not telling jokes.

Some of the men know I'll bury them. If it's late in the day and there's Black Jack being passed around because Mencken Cody or The Broke Rancher sold low-dollar steers for a high-dollar price nobody minds. We're running out of sunsets in White Woman County. Most of our cattle drives are in the graveyards. We drink and joke about what I do. Baker Johnson falling out onto Harper's great toe. Al and his rotgut liver wanting some quiet from Bella.

All summer they put it to me about Clara. How tall she is for her breed. How she's got the same black hair as Maggie. I think they know. Sure they know. But since she's been gone, they don't say much. It's been awhile by now.

We talk about getting through winter until spring against the wind that blows the wheat out of the ground when it's been frozen for thirty days. And stock tanks that ice part way to the bottom overnight. Nothing but hand-pump wells working in Bly. Goddamn.

On the palm of her left hand, Clara had something I couldn't read because of the wrinkles and how she wouldn't open it all the way. I wanted to ask her about it, but I didn't. Sometimes at the Corner Pocket in summer she'd wear clothes so that I could see the edge of a word along her shoulder. And a word on her front where her tits start to begin. Or on her legs when she'd wear a skirt instead of jeans. But I didn't ask about those either. You want to go slow with women if you like them. It's the way you learn to like them. Not that I knew this before. Being with Clara helped. Or maybe it's just becoming who you are when you like what you're doing. *I wish I may, I wish I might.*

You think a lot digging a grave and sitting on the tailgate nights with a Dos Equis Amber. Thinking isn't all bad. Some men won't have it. I like it. It's like coming into good-looking country with your own country still in your head. I do that. Get in my Pick-Me-Up-Truck with Tilly and drive into the Breaks or Sand Hills or the Front Range off the paved roads.

I park in the graveyard of some town more gone than Bly or Blaze, and Tilly sleeps under the truck and I sleep in the back on a bed roll. Every graveyard is different. They all have the same dead, but not the same view. The one in St. Francis has a sign saying watch for rattlesnakes.

I want twenty-six words, Clara tells me one night. We are pushing September into October. I am working at Rose Hill after two days of rain. We don't get much rain in the fall. I'm not digging for somebody just dead, but with Pretty Wilson breathing her last at Pleasant Valley and her relations having asked me to dig the grave when the time comes, I think I'll get it done. I'll put my frame over the hole until I come back to trim it out the day they plant her. Plan ahead to get ahead.

One for each letter of the alphabet, she says. I don't have "A" yet. I got others. I'm up to ten. Maybe I don't have enough body for twenty-six.

What are the others? I said. She says she isn't telling. A girl's got to have some privacies. You got "B"? I asked. She doesn't say anything. I think maybe I don't want to know about "B."

What's that? she says. I've had her help me out of the grave and she's touching the palm of my hand where the brown recluse bit me. It's ragged and rough because I didn't take care of it. A privacy, I said. Fair enough, she says. But make a story for me. Something not true. Sure, I said. Let me think it out so it's good. I'll wait, she says. Why you saving "R?" I asked. She looks away. I want "R" to be for me, but I don't say so.

One day at the Corner Pocket she isn't there. The next night either. Then a whole week of nights not being there. I know where she lives and go by. Her truck isn't there. The house is shut up and nobody answers the door. Not a note. The postman is walking the street and says she's had them hold her mail. Harper comes along in his turbo diesel with his migrant and a backhoe for a grave.

She's not here, he says. I figured as much, I said. You been here before? he says. I tell him she wouldn't let me come over. Not that I asked. You? I said. I guess he doesn't hear me and says he's got to dig the hole for Otto Bond. Then he's off down 4th heading toward Pastor Black's cemetery.

I wish it was better for me and Harper. Maybe it will be when he gets his truck out my lane. He brought my Harley back, but it was a month. I've put it on the porch so Tilly won't chew the tires. When summer comes again I'm thinking to give Clara a ride. We'll do figure eights through the graves, her tendrils blowing in the wind. Maybe she'll help me plant my garden and we'll go fishing together. It will be what we do together days and save nights for digging graves. Work the Corner Pocket like we used to.

When I see her again, I'm going to tell her I going to be buried in Rose Hill. I'll ask Harper to dig my grave but by hand. I'll show her the plots I bought up in the corner. Two plots side by side. Five dollars each. I'll tell her one could be hers if she doesn't have a place of her own. Even if it doesn't work out between us, she could still have my extra plot. That way she'd have a grave to come back to. She wouldn't have to plan ahead.

Maybe it's not what you tell a woman when you're only getting started. Maybe I ought to clean up my place first so she can come over. More than just the garden. The yard. The porch. Get Harper to tow his truck. Make it all handsome like Mr. Badger does in the spring, when he sits on his mound and hoots for the women badgers to take a look-see. Maybe. Mostly I don't know a lot about what I ought to do for myself.

But sometimes I do. I know the catfish I cook for me and Clara are better than the frozen farm fish we get at the Corner Pocket. I know tomatoes out of my garden are better than what you get in the store. I know I cut my graves cleaner than Harper with his backhoe. I know to set the sod aside so when the funeral is done I can lay it out just like it was, and so you don't have to scatter Pasture Number 8 and wait for it to come up. I know to sit on my tailgate in Rose Hill on an August night and watch the lights of Bly blink on, but not so much that you can't see the tracer stars. That's what Clara and I do that first night. There's one, she says. Another over by Levi Johnson's place, I said.

No cares have I to grieve me, no pretty little girls to deceive me, I'm as happy as a lark believe me, as I go rolling, rolling, home. Happy as the day when a sailor gets his pay, as I go rolling, rolling home.

I tell myself I'll have it all in my head when she gets back. She says it should be my song. I think her song must be "Skylark." But I can't get that in my head. Maybe I should. I'll tell her she could have the words on her gravestone if she wants. And I'd have something from her song for me on mine. "By the Light of the Silvery Moon" would be mine. Something to remember her.

I don't live so well, I said to Clara one night. I hear that, she says. I've finished my grave. Maybe she's been with me half a dozen times by now. Leaving from work at the Corner Pocket like that first time. The days are shorter so we got no light to the east just yet. It's not winter in the air, but it's something. Neither do I, she says.

Harper says I'm living in shit, I said. For me as well, she says. She leans back into the bed of the truck and because she's long-legged tall her feet are on the ground and she is tapping out something with one of them. Sing me a song, she says. I'm bad at it, I said. I don't care, she says. I don't know so many, I said. Mostly Willie. Then I think of one from grade school in Blaze.

I was born in Kansas, I was bred in Kansas,
and when I get married, I'll be wed in Kansas.

Clara sings the rest of it with me to the night sky from on her back from where she's at. *She's a sunflower . . .*

It's the last time I saw her before she left for I don't know where.

Winter works for digging graves. You wouldn't think so. But it does. Blowing snow. Frozen dirt. I build a fire over where I'm going to dig. Cottonwood is good, but Elm and Ash are better. Hackberry if it's old. Stack it like a brush pile then splash it with diesel fuel mixed with gasoline. Torch it with my weed burner. Sparks fly. After awhile it settles down.

When I've got a good bed of coals I spread them out and ease my metal frame down over them as a cover. I do this in the afternoon so that when I come back the top is glowing low red and the ground is cooked. All you got to do is get through a foot or so. Even with the grass burned I cut the sod off and make a stack. I stand up the frame and start digging.

I don't need much light. You get used to the dark. When I'm at the bottom, I lie down and look up. The stars from there are brighter and blink harder. Harper says if you dig a hole deep enough you can see the stars in the middle of the day. *Star holes* he calls them. A relative of his on the White Woman used to dig them and let the kids come down and look up. Maybe.

Nights I don't have a good moon, I prop my plywood frame against a nearby tombstone. I paint it white so it will catch starlight or the moon's sliver. I could turn on the parking lights of my truck, but I don't. If you like digging graves at night, you like the dark. Or by the light of the silvery moon, now that I think of it.

You dig winter as well, Clara says the night before she goes away. Yes, I said. How so? she says. I'll show you when the time comes, I said. Tell me, she says. A man's got to have some privacies, I said.

By now I'm out of the hole and I can see she's smiling at what I've said. But I'll know in the end, she says. Trade you, I said. "B" for how I dig in winter. Or why you're saving "R." Maybe, she says and looks away as if to find a shooting star. There, she says. About where you live near Bly. But it isn't there because I'm looking that way as well.

After I find her gone, I start cleaning up. We have some warm days left to us and it's easy. My late tomatoes are still coming in. They're green but you can fry those. Peppers too. Then we have a bad frost, and not much later a blizzard with a foot of wet snow comes through for three days and it's all done for the garden. Good thing I put a tarp over the fold out. Sometimes when I come home, Tilly's sleeping on it if I haven't put her in the house.

Then the snow melts and it turns warm again. Winter warm, not real warm. I go back to cleaning and I think about what kind of story to tell Clara about my brown recluse scar. But it won't come. I think about Clara when I'm digging graves or at the Corner Pocket cooking chicken-fried steaks and catfish. I think about her privacies. About where she's gone. About the songs she sings. I think maybe her story should start and end with my scar, but she'll be everything that's in-between. Songs.

Talk. Words. Only my scar won't be a brown-recluse scar. It'll be a scar that has something to do with her. A woman's got to like you if you put her in a story as if it's a home with words The you've made for her.

Two times I dig winter graves without her. Once I cook chicken-fried steak and hash browns on my metal lid. The other time I grill buffalo burgers. I fix more than my share. I cook early to do the digging early. That way I can go to the Corner Pocket and help out. They usually don't need me much in winter. But I go anyway. Once I sit by the window by the door after they close and down a pint of McCormick's.

It's cold that first grave, but it hasn't been cold enough so that I can't get through the sod once it takes the heat of my fire. Then going down isn't much trouble. It's in January when we've had thirty days of below zero that you have to let your fire cook the ground long enough to roast a hog. In winter, I trade the Dos Equis for pulls of Knob Creek. I like the bottle. It's like a tombstone.

The second grave is about the same kind of thin cold, only with my buffalo burgers instead of chicken-fried steak. Then between Christmas and New Year's, I get two graves. Car wreck. Kids. Brothers. It's deep cold that night. A blizzard coming.

Hello, she says. I'm in the hole of the first grave and it's snowing and blowing up above. I've got my lid on the other one cooking the ground. Maybe I can get both dug the same night. I've been at it since sundown. Hello, she says again.

I heard her come up. Even in the hole with the wind blowing, I hear somebody drive up. It might have been Harper. But I'm making in my mind that it's Clara.

Yo! I said. That's my way of saying hello.

I had thought about it, and what I thought was if she comes back I won't ask her where she's been. Maybe she'll tell me, maybe not.

You need a hand up? she says. Sure, I said. Here, she says. I see she's got on those white-cotton work gloves you wear under leather work gloves when winter comes. Just as I'm about to take her hand she takes off the glove, so I take off mine and she pulls me up. Her hand is warm. How'd you know I was here? I said. Just thought you might be, she says.

It's been at nights in bed that I try out stories about my scar. Some nights my story is when the squeeze chute breaks the time I'm helping Walter Wilcox brand cattle and he catches a piece of iron in his leg. I take a hit of iron myself through my hand and we both go to the hospital in Cottonwood. But Clara might know about Walter Wilcox so I drop it. I want a story that isn't true but could be.

So I start thinking, I'll get the scar doing something to keep her safe. We're in Denver coming out of a motel going for a nice dinner and some punk tries to rob us. He grabs Clara, pulls his Colt, and shoots me through my hand. But quick as Tilly, I've got him on his back with his pistol cocked into his eyeball. I'm asleep before I get to where Clara takes me to the hospital. Or maybe it's back to Blaze because you've got to call the police in Denver if you go to the hospital with a bullet hole in you.

Some nights we go to her house, but since she doesn't want me to see it, maybe not. Then I make the story in summer so she can take care of me on the fold out. That would be good. Summer it is. We head to my place. Even with my bullet hole I drive us back from Denver. She helps turning corners with her left hand on the steering wheel.

Coming out of the grave, I am looking at her and she looks at me, but then she doesn't. I don't much notice how women dress. But this time I do. She's wearing jeans as always, but she's wearing a red plaid coat like a lumber jacket. You don't see those around here. Under that there is a long, yellow scarf wrapped around her neck and then over her shoulder. She's got a white stocking cap pulled down over her ears.

You been back long? I said. Just drove in, she says. Haven't got to the house. You want something to eat? I said looking at the lid over the fire on the next-door grave. I got ribeyes and a bottle of Knob Creek in the truck. Hash browns. Sure, she says. She goes to her truck. Maybe she's cold and wants to get warm. Maybe I should get in with her, but I don't. I go to my truck and turn on my tape deck and listen to Willie: "Help Me Make It Through the Night." Then I get my ribeyes and packets of hash browns. I open my Knob Creek.

Can I come in? she says as she opens the door. Sure, I said. You want a pull? Yes, she says and takes the Knob Creek by the fat of the bottle. How's Tilly? she says. Chews tires, I said. You? she says. I'm working on your song, I said. *No cares have I . . .* We are quiet between us. She takes off her stocking cap and shakes her head so her tendrils fall down.

Have you got my story? she says. Yes, I said. Outside the snow blows in gusts. A foot by morning, I said So I hear, she says. I think to say something but I've lost it. So I go, What's "B"? Harper, she says. Bud. She opens the palm of her left hand and there he is.

That's not what we call him. We call him by his last name. Sometimes Rabbit because of what rabbits do. Not that he brags about it. I'll give him that. But never by his first name. The same for me. Which is why I hope she might save "R" for me because of my last name. The wind gusts so hard we feel the truck rock. We go quiet again. Then.

Would you want to get married? she says, looking at me as she passes the Knob Creek. Me? Yes, she says. To me, she says and laughs and takes the bottle back out of my hand. I'm not married anymore, she says. Where would we live? I said. Maybe buy a place in between us, she says. But both keep our own.

We don't talk. Only breathing. The windows are fogging. I am thinking about her with me on the fold out by the garden in spring. I'm thinking how we've never much touched unless you count her helping me out of the graves or me taking her arm when we cross the street out of the Corner Pocket at night going to my truck. Or how I walk her back to her truck after the sun's come up and open the door and help her in, and how she seems surprised the first time I do that, and I'm surprised at it myself. That kind of touching. Hands mostly. Or once I put my fingers along her cheek under her hair and she closes her eyes. Usually I'm all over them right away to nail them.

I'd be good to you, she says. I know about Maggie. She's my second cousin. I know she gave you the fold out and Tilly and how you wouldn't marry her. She'd have been good to you, but I'll be better. You can live like you want. Or I could help you clean up, if that's what you want. Then we wouldn't have to rent a place in-between. You could be my "R."

I hold out my hand with the scar on it. My story's about us, I said, and how I got shot in Denver protecting you and this is a bullet hole. Then you take care of me on the fold out. Yes, she says. I never had us married, I said.

Skylark, have you anything to say, she sings, taking my hand and looking at it and then out the shotgun window where you can't see anything for the blowing snow. Not even the metal frame which for sure is glowing red and spitting as the snow hits it.

I get out the truck with my ribeyes to toss them on the grill. It's cold. It's not just the wind. It's cold. I go around back and get my spatula to move dinner around. I look at my truck, but I can't see her. I walk over to my first grave and drop in. Not to think. Just to get out of the wind while supper's cooking. But I think anyway. It's not about what I should do with Clara in the truck wanting to get married. It's all kinds of thinking coming at me like snow in gusts. Tilly. *Unfurl*. Bud. I know some places. So do I. Star holes. The Committee to Save the World. My old Harley. Rattlesnakes in the St. Francis Graveyard. And how, when I put new wood in the stove on nights like this, I go outside with Tilly to watch the smoke come out of the chimney and what a pleasure that is, and that I never told Clara that in all the time we talked. And maybe if we were married, she'd go outside with me even when it's blue cold to look at the smoke coming up from the wood stove inside, and then we'd go back and it would be warm.

I hear a door open and shut. Then another. I hear her truck start. I don't move. I hear her turning around. She's by the grave going along though the snow. Then I don't hear her anymore because of the wind.

I say to myself, well, that's that. What? I say to myself. She's gone, I say. You should have said something, I say. I didn't say no, I say. You can't leave it at that, I say. Maggie left and what difference did it make? I say. Maggie never dug a grave with me, I say.

I stop talking and listen to the wind. Nothing but the wind. I think I'll climb out and take a pull of Knob Creek and go home to my shit. Finish the other grave tomorrow.

You want a hand out? she says. This time I don't hear her before what she says. I see her white work glove and she's taken off her cap so her tendrils are flapping around her face. She's next to where the lid is cooking our supper so she's got a glow to her cheek on that side. Sure, I say. She takes off her glove and I take off my glove. Sure, I say.

At least that's what I have myself say for both of us with the wind being the only other sound I hear in the bottom of the grave.

Free Writing

Since this is free writing I am not going to use commas. I don't like commas. I like periods but commas are like yield signs they don't really do all that much. Zu Zu blows them off when she drives. Zu Zu has a Tude.

I'm going to write my free writing about my father and how he quit his job and how that was such a pain to my mother and my sister who was back from college for the summer. We have some goldfish and a cat who is fixed called Mindy. And my grandmother lives above the garage. You probably know some of this. I hope I get an Excellent like I always get in writing. I know I am supposed to learn five things from free writing and keep track of them. I am also going to write some about Bernie and Joel and about my pond. But mainly about my father.

Maybe I shouldn't say my father quit his job because when I said that he freaked out and said he'd been planning this a long time. He calls it LMOL which stands for living his own life for a change. He doesn't include for a change in the initials. My mother calls his being home all the time dropping out only when she talks to my grandmother about it she calls it dropping on like my father is some kind of bomber pilot you see in all the Vietnam programs on television and his being home all the time is like dropping stuff on my mother and her kitchen. I am not going to tell you what my father did before he quit his job that way you can figure it out yourself by reading between the lines which is what you're always telling us to do.

My grandmother asked me the other day if I liked my father and I said yes. Then she asked me if I had anything more to say and I said no. She said that wasn't good. But then she didn't say anything more which I guess means she doesn't much like my father and wants someone to agree with her about it without coming right out and saying so. My father quit his job just about the same time school was over last year so we've had the whole summer together. Most of it anyway. Some kids when they say they like their father are lying but other kids are telling the truth and some kids just don't know what else to say. I don't know why anyone would ask you if you liked your father but it's not the first time I've been asked and I know some other kids are asked as well usually by some relative. I don't know anybody whose mother ever asked them that.

When my father quit his job he said he wanted to be free to pursue other interests. POI he called it. He didn't say quit but he did say other interests and POI. I am also not going to use quotation marks which I know you're supposed to use around words people say. I have this idea I want to claim three free things for free writing and I have just claimed two but it won't be for awhile that I'll know what the third one is. Not telling you what my father did before he quit his job is not one of them. Or some other things about the summer I'm not going to tell about. That's something else.

The first week my father was home I was still in school. The bus drops me up by the Methodist Church in town and I walk home from there. Bernie goes with me part of the way. Joel goes with me the other part of the way and he always has a smoke. That's what he calls them because that's what his father calls them. A smoke. I don't take it. I don't want to smoke. Joel's two grades older. After Bernie leaves and Joel goes up his lane to where his farm is I walk home down a hill in the road and then cut across a field past this pond.

Sometimes I sit by the pond and study the water. I am good at studying the water. Sometimes I talk to the water. I never said anything about this to my mother but once when I was studying the water I must have stayed too long and I saw my mother's car head up the road to town and I knew she was looking for me so I went home and was there when she got back. Where were you she said. I walked by the pond on the way home I said but I didn't say anything about studying the water or about talking to it. I don't know why I'm saying anything about it now except maybe I think in free writing you ought to say something you've never said before. Maybe that's the third free thing I've been looking for. Maybe not. I don't think it is. I'll tell you when I know.

After my father quit his job he said we couldn't spend any money for ten days. He said we had to use up what we had in the house or the planet would go broke. He said there were four things we all had to learn. Zu Zu was home from college and that made four of us if you counted my father but not my grandmother. One thing apiece to learn for each of us Zu Zu said but not to my father because when my father gets this way he doesn't like a joke. Sometimes he likes a joke but not when he doesn't.

My father said the four things were Use It Up. Make Do. Do Without. I can't remember the fourth but you get the picture. He also began planting a vegetable garden and he had a big argument with my mother about it because she wanted to plant flowers there. Zu Zu wanted to plant marijuana. You have to know Zu Zu. She was just kidding. But it freaked out my mother because Zu Zu also once said she was going to get a tattoo of an iguana on her butt which she did not and also that she was going to get an earring in her lip which she did not. Zu Zu calls this mind strafing. My sister's name is Mary but everybody calls her Zu Zu except her teachers who don't know the story about why she's called Zu Zu. My father says Zu Zu has a chronic 'tude which is true because she's always at my father by saying God Dad to dumb things he says. Like when he thought Hip Hop was Hop Hip. God Dad goes Zu Zu only she doesn't say it like God but some other way you'd have to spell it. You have to hear it to spell it.

We are not poor I guess. We don't have to use it up or do without or whatever else it was of the four things. I don't know about money but Zu Zu does and she says we are not poor because she can't get a scholarship to the college where she goes because she didn't get good enough grades in high school and because we're not poor enough. You didn't teach her. We weren't here then.

Anyway we have lots of things and we live in this woods that we bought from Bernie's father off his farm because I guess Bernie's father needed the money. In this woods we built a big house and we came here and I started school even though for a while my father stayed behind to work and only came over on weekends. That was when he had an apartment plus the house where we live now. Sometimes we'd stay at the apartment and drive past our old house just to look at it. My mother didn't want to move and neither did my grandmother. But my grandmother didn't live with us then. She just didn't want us to leave where we lived before because it was close to her. Which is why she came with us.

Nobody around us has a house like we do because ours was designed and built just the way my mother wanted it in order to get her to move. The garage and the man cave which is the basement were built just the way my father wanted them and some parts were built just the way the man who designed the house wanted them. Where my grandmother lives above the garage she got the way she wanted. Something like that. Our house means we're not poor just as much as Zu Zu says we're not poor. We're not rich I don't think. Maybe I should not write about money. Only you said what we wrote had to be true and we couldn't make it up. What if we leave things out. Is it still true if what we put in is true even if I don't put everything in. I should have asked in class.

It was just after I got out of school that my father had a tooth pulled and saved it. He put his tooth in this glass jar with a screw lid on it. He was saving jars and plastic containers for soup and he bought a freezer and moved it into the man cave. This was before he bought a pig and had it cut up and the lamb we called Edna. We just got her skin back before school started. My mother freaked out about the skin and said my father could have it where he is now which is not with us anymore because my mother didn't want it around the house. I am to take it to him when I go there. Also the tooth. But that is my idea. I haven't told my mother about the tooth.

Anyway my father put his tooth in this jar and kept it on his work bench in his man cave because mother said he couldn't have it upstairs even in his office where he makes all these calculations about how much money we can save. He's got a motto above his desk that reads *I'd rather save a buck than earn a buck*. I think he made it up himself. It doesn't sound like the kind of motto you're supposed to learn in Civics from Mr. Schwartz. Or in Sunday school when my mother takes me. Zu Zu won't go. God Mom she says.

When I asked my father about his tooth he told me he was going to save all his body parts from now on. He said he'd wished he saved his appendix when he was a boy and the doctor showed it to him in a jar but he didn't. From now on if he loses something like a tooth or a gall bladder or an intestine he's going to save it in a jar and keep it on his work bench. I thought maybe I should ask him why but I guess I didn't want to know in case my mother asked me. When I asked Zu Zu about it she said it was because my father didn't want to die. Zu Zu's rough.

I asked my father if he was going to save finger nail clippings and when I think about it now it seems like maybe I shouldn't go there but I didn't mean it that way and my father didn't take it that way. He didn't say anything for a moment and then he said when he was a boy his father and grandfather always saved the lead pellets they'd find when they were eating the rabbits they'd shot. That would be my grandfather and my great grandfather. They are both dead and I only remember my grandfather because my father told me a few years ago I was to get his shotgun. I haven't though.

I'm not sure why my father told me about the lead pellets but I didn't say anything although one day when my father was in town I went to the workbench and looked at the jar with the tooth in it and there were no fingernail clippings. There weren't any pellets either. Maybe I thought my father had saved the pellets from when he was a boy and was going to put everything together with his tooth and other body parts that he said he was going to save. When my father came back from town is when he had the freezer.

I don't have a girlfriend. I used to but she didn't know it. I left her a note about how she was my girlfriend under a rock by the pond. The rock is on the bank where the tree fell in. The tree gets turtles on it. The turtles plop into the water when I come along but if I sit there long enough and don't talk they will start to come out. I can only sit there long enough when summer comes because if I did that after school my mother would all the time be going up to the Methodist Church to see if I had been run over and crushed by the school bus. My mother has this imagination about me getting killed. Once I had been dragged by my book bag all the way to the next bus stop which my mother thought was like in Afghanistan. Another time a weirdo picked me up on a motorcycle and took me to a den of iniquity. Zu Zu says Mother wasn't like that with her but that times have changed. Zu Zu says Mother has only two speeds forward: Freaked Out and Totally Freaked Out. FO and TFO Zu Zu calls them. It's from Zu Zu that my father gets his letters for things.

Once I saw a snapping turtle on the bank of the pond that was big as a tire but I didn't tell my mother about it because she would just FO over how it was going to grab me by the pants and haul me out into the middle of the pond and pull me under and I would be dead and my eye balls would rot out of my head after awhile and float to the surface and my mother would see them looking at her and then she'd FOFG. That's my own for Freaked Out For Good. I never told my mother about my girlfriend either. You know her but I'm not going to say who she is. She's still in school but not in our class.

My father has this book. *The Foxfire Book*. He's had it a long time because I remember it was around the house where we lived before. If I say where we lived before you might be able to figure out what my father did without reading between the lines so I'm not going to say only it wasn't like where we live now. It was in a city but not really. You could get to the city by metro which I did but only with my mother. Zu Zu could go by herself and she still has some tickets that she thinks are good but we don't go back there anymore although Zu Zu might because she's got a boyfriend from college who wants her to. I'm old enough to go on the Metro by myself only my mother wouldn't let me because she'd be afraid I'd get accosted which means like being kidnapped by Moonies or homosexuals. She's big on thinking about me being accosted.

My father's Foxfire book has this brown ring where he says he once put a coffee cup. My mother says an old girlfriend gave it to him that's why he still has it. They had this plan about going out west to Kansas someplace and living like Hippies and building a log cabin for the winter but living in a tepee for summer. That's what my mother says. My father just looks off up in the air when my mother says stuff like that. Or when my grandmother says stuff like that. Or when Zu Zu says God Dad. My father doesn't say anything back like Zu Zu will when my mother rags her about something. My father just looks up in the air at like a high spot in the wall but not really. It's like he's trying to look outside the house someplace. If my mother goes on about the Foxfire Woman he'll just puff out his cheeks and blow some air out. But he doesn't get mad or yell or anything.

Bernie says his father's a big yeller and that he beats his mother. Maybe I shouldn't have said that. I've never been in Bernie's house. My mother won't let me go. Not that I've been invited.

When my father put the freezer in his man cave he turned it on just to see if it was going to work and then he turned it off. He said you can't just let it run because that was a waste of money. This was after the ten days we couldn't spend any money but even after that my father kept saying those four things about how we should live which I still can't remember the fourth. Maybe if I write them out it will come back. Do without. Use it up. Make do. That's only three. If my father were here I could ask him about the fourth. I don't want to ask my mother and Zu Zu is back at college. Zu Zu told my mother she has a new boyfriend who is Black with green hair and a ring in his nose and that she is going to bring him home next weekend.

Anyway you don't turn on the freezer until only about a day before you have plenty to put in it because that way it doesn't waste money just staying cold by itself. My father says to me that we are going to have to wait until we get the pig and Edna and even some turkeys he bought from Bernie's dad and some chickens as well and a whole bunch of stuff he's going to get at Sam's one day soon which all happened about a week later. The day before we turned on the freezer and I watched it hum.

The next day Zu Zu and I helped my father fill up the freezer with the pig and Edna and he even froze cheese. I didn't know you could freeze cheese. After it was full my father closed the lid and sat on it like he was happy swinging his legs a little and whistling. My mother and my grandmother had gone to town now that they could spend money. Zu Zu split for the mall. I stayed.

My father whistled pretty good and Zu Zu once told me he had won some state championship whistling contest when he was in like high school. Anyway my father is sitting on his freezer swinging his legs and whistling and that's when he talked to me about what he's doing with his life. LMOL. Not that I asked. I was going to go to the pond to watch the turtles come back on the log after I ran them off. I also wanted to read my note to my girlfriend again. I know what it says I just like to read what I write.

But my father said wait a minute I want to tell you some things about life. He said waste was evil. He said my mother thought evil was something that was inside you and that's why she went to church and prayed. He said my grandmother said that evil was everywhere in everything we did but that was only part of the story and the other part of the story was the good that was everywhere in everything we did but that we needed to ask Jesus to tell us what was good because the Devil would tell us what was evil even if we didn't ask. But my father said he had been thinking about it a long time and that evil was waste because it led to greed and that led to war. He said the Gulf War was because we wasted gasoline and the Vietnam War was because we wanted rubber for our tires which we wasted because we always drove our cars everywhere.

My father had a waste for every war only he skipped some of the wars we studied in school. World War I for example. And the Civil War. He had a waste for World War II but I can't remember what it was. He also said there were religious wars and when he said that he looked up and away like he does when Mother starts in on him. But mainly he said waste was the big problem in life and in his life from now on he wasn't going to waste much. He said waste was like moral rust. MR he said. Here he laughed. MR he said again. I think he knew he was ripping off Zu Zu.

Every once in a while my father would stop talking about waste and start whistling again. I didn't think I was supposed to leave. Before he quit his job he didn't talk to me much only on Saturdays and this wasn't a Saturday so I thought I should stay. I'm not like Zu Zu. I don't mind listening to my father. She's got no time for him. But I didn't mind. He's o.k. When he'd stop whistling he'd start talking about waste again.

He said baking soda was good for waste. You could use baking soda for toothpaste and you could use it under your arms. I knew about using it under your arms because I heard my father and mother get into a big fight about not buying Mennens anymore and my mother told him to go back to work and get a job and stop telling her what to put under her arms. Baking soda was also good for washing your clothes my father said. And if you ever spilled a poison on the floor you could clean it up with baking soda. I could also put baking soda in my tennis shoes which he said my mother ought to buy a size bigger for me and put clumped up paper in the toes until I grow into them. That's when he got going about how many shoes my mother has and how we only need three or four pairs and maybe some boots to get through life. All the rest is waste. He stopped for awhile. I think maybe I should go.

Then he wants to know if I know how many plates we have in the kitchen and I don't. He says we have eighty six flat plates. That's what he calls them. Flat plates. And we have fifty two forks. We have 102 sweaters if you count my grandmother's and Zu Zu's. He's been through the house since we moved and counted all kinds of stuff we don't need. We have twenty two pairs of gloves and some of them only left handed. The reason he says we have such a big house is to store our waste. If we didn't have eighty six flat plates we could have had a smaller house but oh no we've got to have this big house full of plates and shoes and sweaters. By now he's stopped swinging his legs and he's not whistling. He's still sitting on his freezer but he's not whistling.

Do you see this my father says. He pulls out a sheet of paper from his pocket. It is like a page from a magazine only it is folded. This is why I quit. He says quit. This is why I quit. Then he unfolds the paper and holds it out so I can see. There is this picture of a dog looking out at us. See what it says my father says. It says do less have more. This is what's wrong. Everybody wants to have more. A hundred and six flat plates. Three hundred sweaters. Do you know what your uncle said when the stock market crashed a few years ago. He said that was the end of the American Dream. Do you know what he said the American Dream was. He said the American Dream was making a lot of money without having to work for it. That's what he said.

My uncle was in the same office with my father but I don't think that means you can figure out what they did. Then my father doesn't say anything again for awhile. Only he gives me the magazine page with the dog on it and do less have more on it. I kept it. I never understood why a dog would say do less have more.

Then my father asks me what I think. He says he wants to know if I think he's FO or not. He says that means freaked out like I wouldn't know that for myself. FO. What did I think. He sort of laughs like he's supposed to or something but it's not really a laugh.

I don't think much I guess. Not about stuff like waste or church or wars or my mother or father. Mainly I think about what I'm going to do. Like going to the pond. Or what I'm going to say in this free writing. Or trying to guess if Joel is going to have more than one smoke on the way home. I might think about what I'm going to say to the water in the pond but sometimes not. The other day I thought about good and evil because Bernie asked me if I'd do his free writing for him for a dollar. I don't think that's much thinking if you ask me. Anyway I don't know what to say when my father asks me what I think.

But then I think I don't know what I call him. I don't call my father anything. My mother calls him Ted because that is his name but I don't call him that. Bernie calls his father Pops and Joel calls his father Old Man but I've never called my father anything unless it was when I was young. Maybe I called him something funny when I was young because I was the one who called Zu Zu her name because one day she took me to the zoo and after that I just called her that because I wanted to go back so I'd pull on her skirt and say Zoo Zoo. That's what they tell me anyway.

So I don't say anything when my father asks me what I think. Maybe I should have said I think I don't know what to call you but I didn't. So instead I try to whistle but it doesn't come out very well and my father smiles and whistles some himself. It is not something I know. He says it is from a movie about Africa. Very famous. This woman whistles it. Or maybe hums it.

That's when my father says *don't let them outnumber you*. Maybe I should break my rule and put that in quote marks because my father said it a number of times. He has stopped whistling and he is just sitting on the freezer and each time he says *don't let them outnumber you* he either looks at me or he looks away from me like when my mother hits him with the Fox Fire woman and once after he says *don't let them outnumber you* he even puffs out his cheeks. But the last time he says it he's looking at me again. I don't know what he means but maybe if I write it out again it will come to me but I don't want to. Then my father said I could go to the pond. I didn't know he knew about the pond.

I've been thinking. About how you said when we wrote this we could write about anything at all just as long as it really happened only we didn't have to write it like a theme with a beginning middle and end. I've been thinking I'm going to end this before what really happened. I just wanted you to know. Also I've been thinking about the list you said we had to make. The list of five things we learned from free writing. I don't think I can get to five unless I remember all four things my father told me about life and then add something of my own. I don't know what I've learned from this. But maybe if I write about what happened before the end that I'm not going to write about something will come to me. I just want to get another *Excellent* because that's what I've always gotten in writing since we've been here even from Mr. Schwartz who always wants beginnings middles and ends. I know the third thing I am going to claim for free in free writing but I'm not going to tell you even though you've probably guessed it by now. I'll tell you anyway. I'm not going to use question marks. I don't know why it just seems like something not to use. I don't like a question so much if I have to answer it. Joel says in Spanish they are upside down.

Since this is due tomorrow by now I don't have time to write much about everything that happened after my father was sitting on the freezer and whistling and saying all that about not letting them outnumber you. Even if it is before the end of what happened. It is just that I went to the pond because my father said I could. When I got there I went over to the rock where my note to my girlfriend was but it wasn't there anymore. I don't think anybody took it I just think maybe I didn't remember the right rock or that it got washed away with the big rain we had over the summer and maybe now it was in the pond. Maybe the snapping turtle that was going to drag me under until my eyeballs floated up ate it. It was a pretty good note and I liked it because I wrote it. When I get another girlfriend I'll write another note and put it under a bigger rock so I can read it even when I get to the High School.

Anyway I am at the pond talking to the water about waste and trying to whistle. I also try out a few names for my father that I will not write here. I don't like any of them very much but I keep saying them to the water and then I see my mother's car go by on the road. She can't see me where I am. I don't think I have to go home because it's summer so I just stay where I am. After awhile I stop talking to the water and wait for the mud turtles to come out onto the log and they do. I like this because it means you have to sit very still and not do anything but look at them or look at the water or at anything else but you can't talk or move and every time you don't talk or move another mud turtle will come out onto the log like you are calling them by not saying anything. I like that. After awhile the log was full and that's when I heard something down at our house.

You can't really hear all the way from the house to the pond but sometimes you can. Like the time my mother went looking for me you could hear her slam the door to her car only it wasn't a slam just a noise. Then I could hear the car go. This time there was some yelling and I thought Zu Zu had come back the other way and that she was in SLOT. I'm not going to tell you what that means because I don't think free writing means I can use dirty words. Anyway sometimes Zu Zu gets into SLOT and my mother really yells at her and Zu Zu yells right back. I thought that is what it was. Then I hear the car door slam really hard and so do the turtles and they all go off the log. Or maybe they go off the log because I stand up to see if I can see who is leaving if anyone is. Only no one is and then I see Zu Zu's car coming down the road the front way from town so I know she's not in trouble. Trouble is one of the words in SLOT. Then it is quiet for awhile and I think I'll just stay where I am. Maybe the turtles will come back onto the logs or maybe I'll look under some other rocks for my note. I don't know what.

Pretty soon Zu Zu comes up the road just walking and then she comes across the field to where I am. She tells me she knows I come here but she didn't tell anybody. Just when she gets there I see my father's car go up the road not very fast at all.

That's all I want to write. I didn't think if you wrote about things that happened you'd feel like you did when they happened in the first place. Or at least you feel sort of like you did when they happened in the first place. I didn't understand that. Maybe I should have written Bernie's free writing for him then I could have felt like him for a change. Free writing isn't all that free if you come to think about it.

I'll read back over what I've written like you tell us to before we hand it in and maybe I can find some things I've learned even if it's not five. Or if I can't find anything maybe I'll think of something to put in a list just to have it. I don't much like lists because that's what you put in front of colons and I don't like colons because they are like roads signs telling you to look both ways before you pull out.

Stealing

First, I check your dishwasher. Widow women don't use dishwashers. They hide money in them. That's what I did when Mrs. Walters died. Pricilla Walters.

I work at Running Meade Court. Old Folks' Burg. Jack Dogle, the estate buyer, calls you the Nearly Deads. Jack's my brother-in-law. We get on. Sort of.

Lorraine in the front office is always saying *Old age doesn't have to be a wreck. Running Meade's here to make your Golden Years Twenty-Four Carat.* Lorraine's got a big smile. She's tall and young. She's the one who phones me when you're dead. In the Green Shed. It's where I work.

When I get the call your cottage has five days to be cleaned out. That includes the day you're dead. I'm through your door 8 a.m. if 911 hauled you the night before. By then you've got four days. It's in the contract.

If the Bereaved are nearby they can clean you out. Sometimes I work with them. Sort things. Haul trash to the dumpster. Box the Deductibles for Jane Moore at Second Hand Rose. Call Jack to make a Quick Price on whatever's for sale. I get my hourly on Running Meade's clock and maybe a tip from the son. The daughter usually won't tip. Daughters-in-law won't tip for sure. They're all the time sticking things in their purses. Rings. Pearls. Watches. They look for the money, but they don't know the places I know.

The best deal for me is when the Bereaved are in Hong Kong or Texas or Bermuda, and they tell Lorraine to clean Aunt Alice out. They'll get there when they get there. *Be careful. Be careful,* I've heard them say over the speaker phone. *She had Wedgewood from England. And the wine goblets have been in the family since Great Grandfather Baxter ate dinner with General Custer.* You can tell they're having second thoughts. But they don't come back if it's not convenient. Convenience is big these days.

For your "arrangements," Lorraine recommends Eternal Peace. They do Cremations and Full Body Burials. Or they'll store you in a cooler until *the Whole Famm Damnly* gets back. That's what Lorraine says when she's off the phone. *We're to clean out the cottage but Eternal Peace is to put Betty Beulah Land on ice until the Whole Famm Damnly gets back.*

However it works out, somebody's got to go to Eternal Peace and say that's you that's dead. It's the law. Usually Lorraine goes. I just went. For Mrs. Walters. Mostly I don't go. There's a reason.

The Green Shed's got bays with shelves so you can store what won't fit in your cottage. Along the sides of the bays are racks for clothes. Everybody gets a bay whether you use it or not. It's where I put your stuff from your cottage when you're dead. Clocks and mugs of pens and pencils. Flower vases. Candlesticks. Dishes. Silverware. I wash your last dishes. Housekeeping is supposed to do that, but I call the shots when I get the call.

What won't fit on the hangers or shelves I put in boxes. You get charged for the boxes. I magic marker them: *Kitchen. Bath. Bedroom.* I put your name and cottage number on the box, and the date I moved you. I'm organized. I have to be in case I get two calls. *Piggybacked.* That's what Lorraine says. *We got a Piggyback,* she'll say for the second one.

We don't store Consumables. We'll get a tax slip from Jane at Second Hand Rose for what she puts in her Poor Box. We'll do that. But Jane doesn't take frozen food or booze. I take beer.

Jack takes your hard stuff. I take your soups. It's my lunch most days. I heat it on a burner in the Green Shed.

Running Meade charges for me. For the dumpster, too. We're both under *Surcharge. Two boxes of Waste @ $10.00 per box surcharge. Labor, surcharge.* I'm labor. There's mileage on their truck to Second Hand Rose or the dump. If you put a pencil to it, the Bereaved would be better off paying another month's rent on the cottage. That way I don't go through it.

Not that I think one way or the other from what I find of yours. Letters. Pictures. Books. Sometimes I get a laugh. But I don't think one way or other about you. Except for Mrs. Walters. I think about her.

By the time you're boxed, I've got the money. And the Consumables. I like it when you have tuna fish. Chicken of the Sea is my favorite. The frozen food I take home pronto. My freezer is sorted so the oldest stuff is to the top. Ice Cream always goes on top. The Nearly Deads buy the best ice cream. They figure if they eat Lean Cuisine, they can eat real ice cream. Starbuck's Coffee Almond Fudge is my favorite.

I get your Brasso. Baking soda. Salt. Flour for the wife's baking. Onions or potatoes if you've just been to Whole Foods. Rice. Noodles. Coffee. When I've packed a load, I head for home with a stop at Jane's to drop off the cans. Evaporated milk. I don't even know what it is. Beets. I hate beets. Olives. Those tiny onions Jack says you put in martinis. Jane checks the seals on the jars and the date for the cans. You'd be surprised how long a widow woman will keep a can of food. Ten years once for salmon. That's the record. Jane pitched it. What she keeps she puts in the Poor Box by the back door. We've got migrants. By closing time it's empty. Evaporated milk. Martini onions. Gone. Beets. Gone.

Jane knows I take my cut. We go back. High school. We kept at it afterwards, even though we both got married. But we've stopped. Jane's husband works for Eternal Peace. He runs the backhoe that digs the graves. He's the reason I don't go there to see if it's you that's dead. He's the reason Loraine usually goes.

The wife and me, we live out of town, so sometimes when I'm hauling your stuff I'll call her where she works and we meet at home for lunch. We take potluck on the soup. The same for T.V. dinners. I like Swiss steak but the Nearly Deads don't eat much meat. They go for Chinese chicken dishes. They're O.K. But Swiss steak is better.

We have our soup. Then I unload into the basement. My wife doesn't help. She's gotten jumpy about it. Even about the ReGiftables. That's her department. The ReGiftables. She does the dishes and won't look at what I'm bringing in.

I've got shelves in the basement where everything's arranged. Food on one shelf. Products on another. Money I put in glasses and jars with your cottage number on it. Even a shelf for the cat. Pebbles. He's a cut cat. Always sniffing his bowl to see what's in it this time. Picky cut cat if you ask me.

After I get back from lunch, I move what's left of you to your bay. Usually I can get it all in if you've *peeled your onion down.* That's what Jack says when he's buying off you when you first move in and you realize you've got too much stuff for the cottage. *You peeling the onion down?* Sometimes they don't understand.

Jack buys furniture. Plates and silver. Crystal. Tablecloths. Whatever he thinks he can sell in his store. *Old Time Times* it's called. I think he should call it *The Peeled Onion.* But Jack's all business.

"I put it all on the AME," he says. The American Money Escalator. "If they sell Irish Belleek for less than what they paid for it, the AME goes up for me and down for them. But the AME doesn't go anywhere if you don't put something on it. That's America. Running Meade's America. Dead or Nearly Dead."

What Jack won't buy, I take to Second Hand Rose and bring back a tax receipt for the Bereaved. Sometimes I get a tip, even though I'm on Running Meade's clock. If you ask me to take it to Jane, I don't take it to my basement. Usually it's clothes that go to Jane. But even if it's ReGiftables or Consumables, I take them straight to her. Soups too. I put them in the Poor Box myself. Jane gets her lunch from what I bring.

To live at Running Meade you have to have *Deposit Ks*. And you don't get your Ks back if you move out the next day. Not a dime. Your Bereaved don't get it either. Not the money and not the cottage. Or anything you added to the cottage like a deck, or one of those pullout umbrellas over the deck. It's all no longer yours once I've gotten the call. After the *Deposit Ks*, there's the monthly. If you die November 2nd, you owe all of November. They take it right out of your checking account. It's in the Contract.

Most of your Bereaved don't understand and so they're in the office howling at Lorraine. When the lawyers get entangled that makes matters worse. Go back to playing golf in Bermuda, is what I'd tell a Bereaved. The Contract is what you get for not having your mother die in your guest room. Leave the Ks on the AME and forget it.

I don't fool with books except to flip through them for money. That's how I found the note from Mrs. Walters. The note to me. Not really to me. Well, maybe. It's to me. For sure, it's to me. It was in a big dictionary that had its own stand. It's the reason I went to see Mrs. Walters at Eternal Peace. I'll get to that. And about the mink coat.

I hold the books by their spines and give them a shake. *The Whole Famm Damnly* will look through the books for money, but they haven't got a system. I shake the books and sometimes money comes out. It's not like finding a dime on the sidewalk or how once when I was in the Whole Foods parking lot I found a trail of twenty-dollar bills. Finding money in books doesn't have so much luck in it. Maybe it does. It's the shaking them up and down until you find it that's fun. All kinds of stuff comes out. It's like panning for gold.

The woman who lost the twenties didn't know she was losing them until I followed the trail across the parking lot. By then two-hundred-dollars worth of twenties. She told me to keep one, but I wouldn't do it. You don't want to be paid for kindness. That way you lose the pleasure when you think about it later.

Sometimes letters will drop out of the books. I don't read them. There'll be matchbook covers or reading glass tissues, and once a thin silver bookmark. I find slips of paper with lists of things to do. I'll read those. *Call Oliver. Clean sink. Walk. Bank. Library.* I see where they've crossed out what they've done. If it didn't get crossed out, I guess you didn't do it. You can't do everything.

Sometimes I find clippings about the books you've put them in. Mrs. Walters did that. She was the one who had the silver bookmark. Sometimes a book's been autographed. Jane asks me to sort those for her cut.

I find notes like *Make it $30,000 and it's a deal.* Then there was scratching like this guy was trying to get his pen to start. It was on a paper napkin from a bar in New York. Once I found a note that said, *Next time don't be in such a rush.* And on the other side it said, *O.K.* I make myself a story that the *O.K.* was a note that was supposed to be sent back.

I find pictures. Kids at beaches. On horses during a vacation. Pets. People standing around Old Faithful with it going off behind them. Men in uniform next to airplanes. One picture of this man's wife when she was young and not wearing her bathing suit top and on the other side it said, S*outhwest Coast of France, 1954.* I put it back in the book. I put everything I find in your books back. Except the money.

One man had money from all over the world. Jane said I should have kept it in case my wife and I ever went overseas, but I gave it to Lorraine. I give Lorraine half the money I find in the purses and billfolds. *Here Lorraine. Mrs. Jackson's wallet. I found it on the kitchen table. Thank you Randy. Did you find her purse? That too. In the bedroom. Here it is. Thank you Randy. We'll put them in the safe.*

The Bereaved get fifty cents on the dollar from the purses and billfolds. I get a dollar on the dollar from what's in the dishwashers. Or under the tray in the microwave oven. Not under mattresses. Jars they've put way up high behind the cans of soup. In between placemats is good. Under ironing board covers. You look for flat spots. Finders keepers. I'm the Finder. A dollar on the dollar for what I find. Plus ReGiftables and Consumables.

Toilet paper. Clorox. Dishwashing powder. Vitamins. All kinds of pills. I toss those. Kleenex. You'd be surprised how much Kleenex old women have. They're always tucking it up their sleeves. You see it sticking out of them by their wrists, or high on their arms if it's summer. I have a theory that the more Kleenex they put in their sleeves the closer they are to death. When it's sticking out all over them like big white flaky warts, you know you'll be 911 by spring.

I take keys. Master Keys. Yale Keys. Car Keys. House keys. Skeleton keys. Tiny keys that go to suitcases. Keys that go to riding lawn mowers. I sort them into jars. Big Keys. Little Keys. Sometimes nights in my basement I put the keys on my workbench and make of a story about them. How the husband died with his John Deere-riding-lawn-mower key in his jean pocket, and when the hospital returned his clothes his widow washed the jeans and the key came out in the laundry. Then she put the key in a jar, and when her kids moved her into Running Meade, they moved the jar as well. That kind of story.

My wife says it's stealing what I do. I say maybe taking the money is stealing. But not the Scrub-So-Soft and Lubriderm. Not the keys. Not what we give our daughters for coming to see us. Or what's in the ReGift Drawer. Like dish towels if they're in a set with fancy pot-holders and a kitchen apron. My wife thinks giving that to her sister for a birthday isn't stealing. Maybe the money is stealing.

But if the money's stealing, then it's all stealing. Not just the money. The money and the Lubriderm. The soup. The keys. The Starbuck's ice cream. It's all stealing.

Jane takes your laundry soap for the Poor Box. The Pine Sol. The soups. She sells your scarves and purses you never took out of the boxes. But not to the poor. There'd be too high a price on them for the poor. But I'm poor if you pencil me against the Nearly Deads. My wife works a job at the county and I cut grass weekends in the summer. I plow snow in winter. We got medical bills. I put one daughter through state college and the other one halfway through before she got knocked up. The house is mortgaged once to the bank, and again to Jack. Not that the bank knows about Jack. I'm not poor like the Migrants. I know that. It's just I'm getting first pick. Is that stealing? If somebody else gets second pick, is that stealing? What about Jack's AME? Think about it.

Fifty cents on the dollar out of the purses might be stealing. It might be. But a dollar on the dollar out of the dishwasher might not be. For sure I can't tell my wife a thing about what's stealing and what's not. We stopped talking about it. Until I brought home the mink coat.

It was in Mrs. Walter's attic. I knew her because she'd call me at the Green Shed and say that Nike was on the loose. *I'll find Nike, Mrs. Walters. I'll find Nike.* He never went far. He was a Pug. A low-to-the-ground dog. Always running away.

After Mrs. Walters died, I took him to the pound. You get charged for that too. The *Puff of Smoke Pound*, Lorraine calls it. Mainly your Nearly Deads have cats. I'm to take those to the pound but I don't. I put them out by the county lake. Only once I kept Pebbles.

By the time I find Nike, Mrs. Walters is walking over. I have these two aluminum folding chairs from one of the bays years ago. She pats Nike and rests herself. We don't talk much except about the headline news or the weather. Every once in awhile she looks at the Bays filled with stuff Jack hasn't put on the

AME and says, *Getting and Spending, Getting and Spending*, like it was something she'd read in a book or the newspaper.

Mrs. Walters died during the night the last time she came over to get Nike. The light was blinking on the phone when I opened the Green Shed. I knew what it meant. I just didn't know who.

Right after 911 hauled her, Lorraine called me and said Sales had some Nearly Deads who wanted to move in *Pronto*.

Get her out so Housekeeping and Painting can get in. Don't store it. There's no Whole Famm Damnly. Call Jack and get a Quick Cash Price right out of the cottage. Take the rest to Second Hand Rose or toss it. Keep track of the dumpster loads for the Surcharges.

Mrs. Walter had no Bereaved and no will, which means the county gets it all. When that happens, Running Meade's lawyers figure how to bill the B-Jesus out of your estate for all kinds of things. Like me taking Nike to the pound.

I opened Mrs. Walters's cottage and looked for the money. There was twenty dollars in her purse, and maybe it was because of Nike and how we used to sit together that I gave it all to Lorraine even though it was two tens. *Thank you, Randy.* No other money in the usual places.

I called Jack. I took Nike to the pound and went back to Running Meade. When Jack showed up, he made a Quick Cash Price for what he wanted and went to the office to pay Lorraine. I spent the afternoon hauling for Jack on Running Meade's clock. Then I hauled two loads to the dumpster.

At quitting time I locked the cottage. I took my cut of Consumables. It wasn't much. Toilet paper. Janitor in a Drum that still had a sticker on it from when Mrs. Walters moved into Running Meade. Glass Plus. Brillo. A packet of fancy soaps from France I figured my wife could ReGift. Band-Aids and Rolaids and rubbing alcohol from her medicine cabinet. But not her prescriptions. They were on the kitchen table in a row by her Days-of-the-Week pill box. I tossed those.

The next morning I made a run to Jane with two boxes of autographed books, all of them to *Pricilla Walters*. Some of the writers wrote notes as if they were friends.

After Jane's, I went back to the cottage and remembered I hadn't checked the attic. Usually we don't bother with attics unless they're finished. You have to go up this ladder in the utility room, and be careful to walk across the floor joists or you'll go through the ceiling. One guy did that with a birthday present he'd hidden for his wife and fell through and died. Lorraine said it was a bud vase. *A crystal bud vase*, she kept saying. *With a single rose in it. The vase didn't even break.* It happened before I started at Running Meade.

I go up the ladder and through the lift panel and pull the chain on the light. Nothing. Only planking. I walk across the floor joists to have a look-see under the eaves. Nothing. I'm about to go back down when I think, what's that over by the gas vent? And it's a mink coat. Only I don't know it's a mink coat because it's in a box, so I don't know what it is until I get it down the ladder into the utility room. Then it's a mink coat.

I go to the Green Shed and call the wife and say we'll have lunch. Then I sit on one of my folding chairs and put the coat on the other. I am trying to make a story that goes with the coat being in the attic. But nothing comes into my head. I think it's not Mrs. Walters' coat because all the time I knew her she was too old to be going up and down the utility ladder.

What's this? my wife says. *A Mink Coat* I say. *It's from . . . Don't tell me*, she says. *I don't want to know. Try it on*, I say. *No*, she says. *Take it back or Lorraine will be out here and find all the stuff you've got in the basement. The money and everything. Put it back! Put it back! We'll go to jail unless you put it back.* My wife won't even let me eat lunch she so hot about it. *Put it back!*

I take the coat and think maybe I should just drive to the cottage and go up the utility ladder and leave it where I found it. Or maybe give it to Lorraine. But I don't. What good's a mink coat in an attic where nobody knows it's there? And Lorraine would just take it for herself. Jack would put a Quick Cash Price on it and wait for winter and up it ten times. Everybody gets a cut but me unless my wife will have it. And she won't.

On the way to town I drive the road to the county lake. I'm stalling. I don't know what to do, but I think if I drive slowly, I'll figure it out. I stop where I let out the cats. Nobody's around. Just me and picnic tables and trash cans. Ducks on the lake.

I sit in the truck. Then I get out and put on the coat. I'm not big, so I can get into it. I don't know why I'm doing this, only once I saw an advertisement in a magazine with Joe Namath wearing a mink coat. I like Joe Namath. Anyway, I put the coat on. That's when I find the note. In the pocket. It's the second note I've found from Mrs. Walters since she died. The one I find in the pocket of the mink says: *This is not my coat. I do not know how to give it back*. It was signed *Pricilla Walters*, just like the note from her I found in the dictionary. I'll get to that. Same handwriting.

Now I got a mink coat my wife doesn't want, and I got a note out of the pocket from Pricilla Walters. Plus the first note from the dictionary before I found the mink coat.

Jack drives up. Maybe he's been to a farmhouse to buy collectibles. Or maybe he's got some Strange out this way. I think he does. I think I know her. Then I remember there's an auction in Wells on Wednesdays, and he's taking the back road to town. He stops. I'm standing there in Mrs. Walters' mink .

"What's up?" he points at the coat.

"I found it," I say.

"At Running Meade?" he says.

"Yes."

"The cottage you just emptied?" he says.

"Yes."

"You taking it?" he says. "For Laura?" Just then somebody we both don't know goes by in a pickup. Migrant man.

"Laura doesn't want it," I say.

"Why not?"

"Just doesn't."

"You need a price?" he says. He gives the sleeve a feel. "It looks nice on you." He winks. I should tell him to get fucked, but he's not all bad.

"You think so?" I wink back.

"A quarter," he says. "No one has to know."

He pulls out his wad and peels off two-fifty. I look at the money. Something is happening to me. Just looking at the money, something is happening.

"I don't think so," I say.

"Three?" he says.

"It's not the money," I say.

"What's not the money?" Jack says. "Laura doesn't want it. Lorraine doesn't know about it. It's a clean deal."

"Maybe it's not right to sell it."

"What are you saying?"

"It's not mine," I say.

"Everything out of Running Meade's not yours," Jack says.

"It's stealing," I say. Jack looks at me like I'm not who I am.

I'm standing there talking to Jack and thinking about Mrs. Walters' note in the dictionary when I was looking for money and found a slip of paper. *I know what you do when we die.* It was signed *Pricilla Walters.* Underneath her name she had written: *ISTMP.* I put the note in my wallet. I am thinking all this standing by the picnic table with Mrs. Walter's mink on. I get out my wallet and Jack's figures I'm going to take his money, but I'm not.

"What's this?" he says. I hand him the note from the dictionary.

"It's to us," I say. "I found it in her cottage."

He gives it a glance. Then hands it back.

"So what if she knows," he says. "She's bye-bye."

"Maybe not," I say. I don't know what I'm saying.

"You think she's not bye-bye," says Jack, and I can see he's inching away like me wearing the coat in the middle of nowhere by myself was something he shouldn't have joked about. "She's dead, right? 911 dead. On the slab in the cooler at Eternal Peace."

"She's dead," I say. "But what she says isn't."

"She's talking to you," Jack says. "I got a license for what I do. I pay taxes. I took a course in being an estate broker. I got my certificate on the wall. You're the one she's talking to here. It's your cut she's talking about. You want to sell the coat or what?"

I don't say anything. Then I say *O.K.* It seemed like what I should say with Jack standing there holding out three hundred dollars and me wearing Mrs. Walter' mink. At least I get my cut.

I take the coat off and give it to Jack and take the money. Then I hand the other note to him. The one about the coat not being Mrs. Walters's that was in the pocket.

"What's this?" he says.

He reads it, then tears it to pieces and pitches it on the ground.

"Maybe the coat was stolen," I say.

"You're getting . . . " and I can't hear what he says because another truck goes by.

"Maybe," I say, but I don't know what I've agreed to.

"I got to get going," Jack says as he climbs in his truck with the mink. We drive to town. I'm behind.

I don't feel good. I'm trying to think it through. I got my basement full of keys and Scrub-So-Soft and water glasses of money and paper towels. Upstairs in the guest room there's French Soaps and potholders and perfume for ReGifting. Then there's this mink coat I just sold to Jack even though it wasn't mine.

Jack's pulls into Second Hand Rose and I know he's going to put the coat on consignment instead of waiting for winter. *I'll buy it back,* I say out loud to myself in the truck. I'm behind him in the parking lot. I honk. He sees it's me.

"I'll buy it back," I yell as I get out. He's walking toward Jane's with the coat.

"Five hundred quick cash price," he says without stopping.

"Here's your three hundred," I say catching up with him. "Follow me to the house and I'll get the rest." He stops.

He's looking at me like I'm fucking nuts. He's looking at me like he'll never think I'm anything but fucking nuts no matter how long we both live. Like maybe I was going to pull down my pants and beat my meat out there by the county lake with Mrs. Walters' coat on when he drove up.

"Jesus," he says.

We get in our trucks and drive to the house. He stays in the kitchen while I go into the basement and get the money out of the water glasses. I take a ten from one glass, a twenty from another and so on, until I get the two hundred. When I come up I hand him the money and he hands me the coat.

"I think you're losing it," he says.

I know that's not what he said when the truck went by at the lake, and I wonder if he'll tell Laura about all this or if he'll just let it go.

"I'm quitting Running Meade," I say.

"I can't talk to you," he says and walks out the door. The phone is ringing but I don't answer it.

I go into my basement with the coat. I put it on the bench where I sort stuff. I look at my Consumables. I open the freezer and look at the T.V. dinners and the ice cream and all. I put Mrs. Walters' note to me in her coat pocket.

Then I hear the door open upstairs. My wife calls, *Randy*. I say I'm in the basement. She comes down. Part way. She sits on the stairs. She says Lorraine has called her to see what's up.

"You sick? I talked to Jack and he said . . . "

"I'm not going back to work," I say.

"What's with the coat?" she says. "I told you . . . "

"I bought it."

"You bought it?"

"It's yours," I say.

"I don't want it," she says. But she's looking at it.

"I didn't steal it," I say. "I bought it."

"What do you mean you're not going back?" she says. "Lorraine's looking for you. She wants you to go to Eternal Peace and tell them it's the woman who died the other night that's there. She says you knew her."

"I'm not going back."

"You sick?" she says. "Jane says you stopped there with Jack then drove off. Then Jack said . . . "

She comes the rest of the way down the stairs. It's the first time she's been all the way down for a year. Maybe more. She takes the coat off my bench and holds it out, then puts it on. She looks good in it. I think my wife looks very good in it.

"It's never been worn," she says. "What's this?" She's found Mrs. Walters' note in the pocket. "What's it mean, she knows what you do?" My wife's taking off the coat. "I don't want it," she says. "Not even if you paid for it." But she's holding it.

Then she looks around the basement at my shelves and how neatly I've got it all organized. Maybe she's going to say we should take the money to Lorraine so we can keep the rest and not call it stealing. Maybe she's waiting for me to say it.

"I'm not going back never," I say. "I'll take the money to Lorraine, if that's what you're thinking."

"What about the rest of it?" she says. She's got the coat over her arm and looking around.

"I don't know," I say.

"I had some of the ReGifts planned for Christmas," she says.

She puts the coat back on and looks at the note from the pocket and reads it again.

"What do you think it means below where she signed?" I say. "*ISTMP.*"

"'I Stopped Taking My Pills,'" my wife says as she moves so the coat settles over her. She looks at herself over her shoulder down the back.

"How'd you figure that so quickly?" I say.

"It just came to me," she says.

I walk up the stairs and out the door to my truck. I drive to Eternal Peace to tell them it's Mrs. Pricilla Walters they got. She was on a cart behind a curtain. I found her on my own because nobody was around. I wanted to talk to her, but I was afraid somebody would come along and it would be like wearing her mink when Jack drove up.

I didn't know what I'd say, but I knew once I got started I'd say that I knew her note in the dictionary was for me. And how I gave all twenty dollars from her purse to Lorraine. That I was going to get Nike out of the pound before they puffed him. That Nike and Pebbles would just have to get along. How I missed her sitting with me in the Green Shed. Was it true about *ISTMP*? How did she get the coat up in the attic? Whose coat is it anyway? How does she know what I do when you're dead? Didn't she ever take a cut? Why were all those books signed to her? What should I do with what I've stolen? The money. The Consumables we have for lunch and supper. The ReGiftables my wife has planned for Christmas. The mink coat that's not hers. What should I do?

But I don't say anything. Pretty soon along comes this woman who wants to know if I am Randy and can I identify The Deceased. I tell her The Deceased is Mrs. Pricilla Walters of Running Meade Court. She writes it down on a clipboard and I have to sign where she's put an X. Then because I don't leave, she asks if there is anything else. I can't talk to Mrs. Walters like I want to, so I say no.

I've quit Running Meade. I mow lawns. Plow snow in the winter. I'm spending down the money out of the glasses. Gas. Groceries. We pay Jack on the second mortgage. The cash won't last the year. But we got our Consumables. ReGifts. Nike is with us. He and Pebbles don't get along. My wife still works for the county. She won't talk to me about anything. Some days in my basement I think I should give it all back, but everybody's dead. And like Mrs. Walters said about the mink, I don't know how. Only I can't think she stole it. I've made stories about whose coat it is and how she got it in the attic, and why she couldn't give it back, and nowhere in my stories does Mrs. Walters steal it.

Not like me. When the girls open a present from the bays, I know it's stolen goods we've made a gift of. When the wife and me have T.V. Swiss steak for dinner, I know we're eating stolen food. And the dish soap she uses to wash up. The mink coat she won't wear except to take it out now and then to look at herself in the mirror. Beer, when I have one with a ball game on the Television I've got in my basement. A house full of stealing. Not that it gets it off my mind to say so to myself.

When the World Was Young and the Death of Bird Four

The Rushing of Seasons

Their tax man told Anne the only safe ("safe": he repeated the word: "safe!") way to deduct even part of their yearly July and August trip to Paris was for her to make "French Paintings," with "French titles," and "French subjects." Like nudes. Or cheese and fruit on tables. Or wine bottles on tables: *Chèvre Avec Femme*, Anne thought. Brie with legs. Nudes with legs. Wine with legs. On tables with legs. Herself with legs.

"Write the titles on the back of the paintings," he said. "It might be better if you write them in French, even if you have to get someone to help you. Think of your painting as a document for the IRS. If you sell one, take a picture of it. Document everything. That way you'll be safe. Document everything. Tell Roy. He'll understand."

On the way home she stopped at the farmer's market to buy strawberries for dessert that night. They were being shipped from North Carolina and expensive, and not all that good.

"'Seven francs a kilo,'" Roy said, looking at the strawberries.

"What?" Anne said.

"It's a Sinatra song my parents used to listen to," he said. "Something about strawberries costing seven francs a kilo."

"I don't know it," she said.

"What did Tax Ted say?" Roy said.

"That I should paint Paris at night. Then to be safe, title it 'Paris at Night.'"

"Then take a picture of it?"

"Yes," she said.

"I told you so," he said. "What else?"

"That we'd probably be audited for last year, and that we'd probably have to pay. Both interest and penalties."

"I doubt that," Roy said. But he frowned. Then he began to look for the bruised or green strawberries in the carton, taking them out and setting them aside, saying:

"You should wait for the local ones to come in. Don't rush the season. Everything in its own good time."

What to Do with Bird Four?

What to do with Bird Four while they were in Paris? Last year Bird Three died. The year before, both Bird Two and the cat died. The year before that, Bird Two made it through, but their first year in Paris Bird One had died. Roy said he expected to open up *International Herald Tribune* and read of mass pet deaths in America. At least Bird Three had died while they were home.

Anne's mother had given them their first canary (named "Yellow") the year before they started going to Paris. Joy-filled, her mother would say when she came into their house.

"They make a place so joy-filled. Besides, canaries were used in your grandfather's mines to detect some kind of nasty gas. Put them in the basement to detect radon. Isn't it radon in basements these days? Leave the bird in your studio overnight to see if it dies. But don't tell me. I don't want to know about dead birds. And have Roy build you a studio above ground. He's got the money."

One summer day when Roy was cleaning the cage, Yellow flew out and was gone.

"I wonder what Doctor Freud would say," Roy said. Anne said she didn't think it was very funny. Her mother said she'd get them another "Yellow."

"No need to change names if you don't change species," she said to Roy. "Anne's father and I had four toy boxers all named Max." When she brought them the second canary is when Roy started numbering them.

"The least she can do is take care of them when we're gone," Roy said.

But Anne's mother wouldn't. So the first summer they arranged for a college girl down the street to house-sit. Late one night in Paris the phone in the apartment they'd rented rang and Bird One was dead: Sorry. Really.

"Belly up," Roy said the next morning. "So Yellow Radon Bird One went belly up. I hope Coed Connie didn't try to grind it down the garbage disposal."

A year later, the same girl called the Paris apartment at about the same time to reassure them that Bird Two was doing just fine: How was France? It's very hot in Washington. But the house was cool because we've kept the air conditioner going. Did they mind if her boyfriend stayed a few weeks? He was studying modern Europe in college and knew all about Paris and the war and how Hitler kept asking *Is it burning? Is it burning?* The plants were fine. Really. The bird was fine. Really. The cat is awesome.

The third summer, Bird Two died; by then they had hired a cleaning lady to water the plants and feed both the bird and the cat. Roy asked the neighbors to watch for House-Emptying U-Haul Trailers, or columns of smoke rising through the roof, or streams of water coming down the driveway. Everybody said everything would be fine. Go to Paris. Have fun. The cleaning lady didn't call about the death of Bird Two; it just wasn't there when they got home.

"At least she cleaned the cage," Roy said. It was the neighbors who told them the cat had been run over by a Rive Gauche van. You know, the new caterer that everybody is using. We didn't want to spoil Paris by calling about a dead cat. It was painless. We buried her by your apple tree.

Her mother promised that she would give them another canary for Anne's birthday in October. But she said that they must take better care of them. Two dead birds in three years, not counting the one that flew away. Not much joy in that. As for the cat, her mother didn't like cats. They were sneaky: You didn't feed the dead birds to the cat did you?

"Please don't bother about another bird, Mother," Anne said.

"What's the bother?" said her mother. But Anne's birthday came and went with no bird. In fact, no gift.

"Don't ask," Roy said. "It's a blessing." Her mother gave them Bird Three for Christmas, but it died the next day.

"I tell you Bird Three is belly up," Roy said to Anne, as she was taking a shower. "Maybe there's radon in the living room."

"I don't want to hear about it," said Anne, not turning off the water.

"Let's just have it stuffed. Your mother will never know," Roy said. "We'll find an old Montavani album and crank up the turntable when she comes in and she'll think it's the bird singing. Montavani is so joy-filled."

A week later her mother gave them Yellow Bird Four. The previous bird was "defective," she said. The replacement bird was free. It was the advantage of dealing with the local pet store. They stood by their birds.

The Car Is on the Table

"Do you want to go to Paris again this year—or not," Roy said from the couch in the living room where he has settled down with *Newsweek*. There was an edge to his question. In previous years when Anne had expressed even the most reasonable restraint about leaving the house, the cat, the bird, the . . . what? . . . the routine?, Roy had become impatient with her in just the way she could now hear.

"I do, but I don't want to worry," she said. She had expressed this reservation before, and she wondered if he'd say: *You said that last year. And the year before that. Here I go and arrange the business so I can take off for two months in order for you to get a little of Paris under your belt for your painting, and you worry about birds and cats and the washing machine hoses breaking. We could stay home and build a swimming pool and save money.* But he didn't say anything.

It was as if restraint were growing inside her, not a spiritual or psychological thing, but more like bones or fat or blood vessels or organs. A full body X-ray would show a spare organ somewhere between her heart and her pelvis, dark and quivering. What is that? a doctor says. Restraint, says the nurse without hesitation. She puts a hand on Anne's head.

Anne had been the one who suggested Paris. It would be good for them. Good for their marriage. A change of pace. A way of putting their lives back together. That kind of self-help thinking. Roy's business—his company drilled "test holes" for road and bridge builders—had done quite well in recent years and as a result he could split the duties with his partner George, who was "into boats." Two months vacation (August and September for themselves; October and June for George and Sally), plus the security of a fully funded retirement plan, were just two perks test holes had provided them: a Stretch Volvo (Roy's phrase here), quota colleges for the kids, business class tickets on flights to France, a yard man to go with the cleaning lady, "power shopping for the wife," the backs of paintings as documents for the IRS—it was all adding up. Strawberries out of season.

"We could let the kids use the house," he finally said. "They might enjoy the change, and they'd take care of it. Cut the grass. It would be a cheap vacation for them." He got up from the couch and walked into the kitchen where she was sitting at the table, cutting the green and white out of the strawberries.

"They have their own homes," she said.

"Well, then?" he said, the edge out of his voice. He put down *Newsweek* and studied the car ad on the inside cover. "George

Will was good this week. Better than what's-her-face last week. She wobbles. George never wobbles." He sat down.

"I don't know," Anne said. "I don't know what to say."

"*Le voiture est sur la table*," he said.

"You just said the car is on the table," she said, thinking of the time he tried to buy some tickets for the train to Versailles, but had—according to Fredericka—ordered two seats of stomach bile. He pointed at the picture of the car in the *Newsweek* advertisement.

"I know what I said," he said. *La*, not *le*, she thought to say, but did not.

Socrates Is a Man

People with fewer choices live better lives. It was the kind of thought she could not test on Roy. Not that he wouldn't talk about ideas ("topics" he called them), it was that they had to be impersonal: distant, listed. Served like restaurant fare. Or off the "S.S. Lists" (Saturday/Sunday Lists) he made for himself: The nature of screen doors. The value of riding lawn mowers. The essence of "pressure treated" wood. Or—to give Roy his due—more general topics from George Will's column: the dinner special tonight might be what the Christian Coalition is doing to the Republican Party. A topic for talk. Not an idea to be tested through. *People with fewer choices lead better lives.* Roy would cut it to the bone: *You have fewer choices when you have less money? Do you want to be poor? Will you be happier poor? You'll have fewer choices.*

Life for Roy was not a matter of choices, but a matter of arranging for choices. When you had two, or three, or four options, you could go to work on them. If Anne didn't want to accept George and Bella's invitation to spend a weekend at their beach house in Delaware, that was fine. What then?: asked not in anger. Not in disappointment. Just: What then? The movies?

The concert at the college? A walk? Nothing? Nothing was fine with Roy as long as nothing was decided on. Something could come of nothing: *Let me know.* Then he'd head out to mow the lawn, or tinker with the car, or run some errand in the nearby shopping center, as often as not coming home with a specialty bread for dinner that night, or flowers for the table. And as full of good cheer in his own fashion as her mother was in hers: *I thought you might enjoy some daisies. The bread is still warm. What's cooking: chicken, wanna neck? I know small Bordeaux.*

But for Anne, a life of lists and topics and choices was growing more than vaguely dissatisfying. It reminded her of college logic and how over-and-done-with-it those Monday-Wednesday-Friday 10:30 syllogisms had seemed to her (in spite of the talk-until-dawn-crush she and her roommate Sara had on Professor Gassett). *"All men are mortal"* led in two quick steps to the death of Socrates, complete with Professor Gassett's chalk line coffin lid drawn over the conclusion.

Was that all? Life in major and minor premises? And then the line on the black board. What about the way she felt? What had become of the premises of what was to become of her? What about happiness? What about movies where she cried? Where was the premise that was Roy? And two children? And Paris? Her father's death? What about the Uccello painting with all its baby-faced soldiers she had seen projected in her art history class in the very same room the hour before logic? What conclusions have there been since the death of Socrates? What lines drawn on what blackboards? What about lean, handsome, worldly Professor Gassatt and his hint of an accent? And the way he'd put his right hand on the top of his head when you'd ask him a question. And how his long fingers would disappear into the black boil of rich hair as he'd lean toward you with the answer: *The conclusion of the syllogism is the ultimate truth of its premises, Miss Johnson. Do you understand?*
She did not.

The Apartment in Paris Was a Gift

"I sometimes wondered," Fredericka says, "how I'd feel about meeting you again."

"I never did," Roy says.

"Sweet of you to say," she says. Then Fredericka says something Anne cannot hear from the bedroom.

"I didn't mean it that way," he says. "It's just that I don't think about meeting people from ye olden college days. I do think about ye olden college days, however. I think about the time we . . . "

"I don't," Fredericka says.

"Maybe that's the difference between men and women," he says.

"I don't believe in the differences."

Anne hears a pause between them. Outside there is the noise of the traffic, and from farther away a loud cheer. Maybe one of the street theater acts has come to an end on Pont des Arts: a mime dying; a diver off the bridge into the Seine; the man (or is it a woman?) on stilts doing a falling bow.

"Jane tells me you're a trapper in Kansas," Roy says.

"Not really," Fredericka says. "Something like that, though."

"And a Communist."

"Not really," she says. "But something like that."

"What are you then?" he says.

"What do I know?" she says. There is another pause. Anne wonders if Fredericka is smiling, and if so, is there irony in it? If there is a sfumato to it? She doesn't know her well enough to know. She hears them talk on, but not about much. Then she falls asleep.

The apartment in Paris was a gift. They could use it July and August as long as they paid the cleaning lady and the electric bill. Roy's sister Jane had married a French lawyer and they had settled on Place Dauphine in the late '70s. In the summer they went to the Dordogne where they lived—if the pictures on the dressers were any indication—in a château roughly (as Roy put it) the size of the Chevy Chase Club.

Anne spent her Paris days making paintings on a portable Italian easel; Roy spent his reading the *International Herald Tribune* and crime novels, and "scouting restaurants" for the evening meal: *It is my calling to walk the Boulevards of Paris in search of a meal and a bottle of vino,* he'd say as he'd head out in some direction or the other, more often than not coming back late in the afternoon with a discovery just as if he'd come back from the shopping center with a warm loaf of bread: *Tonight we dine at Le Caveau du Palais, which, if you will notice, is just across the park. A Bulls throw from here.*

"*Boules,*" said Anne, whose French improved with each visit, but who noticed little such movement in Roy's: *Où est la café. Où se trouve la Louvre. Le fleur est sur la table.*

Place Dauphine had a catch: Roy's college girlfriend had been—and still was—a good friend of his sister's and used the apartment on her summer wanderings throughout Europe. Not so much to live in, Anne was assured (and reassured), but only to "park herself and a few of her things now and then." Fredericka would be in the small bedroom off the kitchen. She had her own key. And while she was more than a bit of an eccentric what with her politics and her writing and her pilgrimages, she would not be any trouble.

Anne did not want to give much thought to what might or might not have transpired between Roy and Fredericka twenty some years before. During her marriage there had been a woman in Roy's life to concern herself about. Jealousy had bled her dry. Something in her died: all the usual clichés in spite of them being the usual clichés. Trust was trashed.

When they met Fredericka in Paris that first summer, Fredericka made it a point to be especially pleasant and courteous to Anne. No, she would not be staying long, just a few days, then she'd be taking the train to the Dordogne to visit Jane; then on to Spain by bus.

"I know Paris pretty well," said Fredricka to Anne, "and my French is decent. So if you'd like to use me as a walking *Plan de Paris* before I go, let me know. I'd enjoy it."

Anne thanked her, and while she fully intended to take Fredericka up on her offer, she never got around to it. Instead she walked to the Louvre and looked at the Uccello she had seen in the art history class the hour before Socrates and his syllogisms.

The second summer (and the non Death of Bird Two) Fredericka returned to the apartment with a political Frenchman and the two of them sat up all night in the kitchen talking French about what Anne imagined was the socialist agenda in Eastern Europe (a scene out of *Reds*, Anne thought, even as it was going on). The third summer Fredericka came before and after they were in Paris. And last summer the three of them drank too much wine one night in the apartment and said some things to each other they should not have.

Are We Going to Paris?: A Topic for Conversation

"Did Ted really say something about being audited?" Roy said at dinner.

"No," Anne said.

"Why did you tell me that?" he said.

"I was upset," she said.

"'Upset'?" he said. "Why?"

"I don't know," she said. "Let it drop."

"Are we going to Paris this summer?" he said. "I'd like to know, because if we're not . . . "

"I don't know," she said. "I don't think so."

"Why not?"

"You don't much like it, so why should you care?" She could feel something going on inside her. What was it?

"I like it," he said. "You're a grump this evening. *Le fleur est sur la table.*"

"Have you heard from Jane if Fredericka will be there?" she said.

"I have not," he said. "She probably will. What difference does that make?"

"It wasn't such a pretty scene last year," she said. "I'm surprised we get to use the place at all if she told your sister what happened."

"Blood is thicker than water," he said. "Or wine. We were all drunk."

"Speak for yourself," Anne said, although with less velocity than she felt entitled to.

"It wasn't her business to butt into my life," said Roy.

"Or mine?"

"Yours either."

The next week Bird Four died.

When the World Was Young

"When you think about him, what do you think about?" says her roommate Sara one night.

"I think about his black hair," Anne says. "I think about his green eyes. I think about his voice. His accent."

"I think about him making love to me," Sara says.

"I don't think about *that*," Anne says.

Her roommate's full name was Sara Johnson. Johnson was Anne's last name as well. They had fun telling people they were sisters. The following year, Sara transferred. Or dropped out. Anne never knew which. They hadn't kept in touch over the summer, and their names and their crush on Professor Gassatt aside, they had pretty much gone their separate ways in college. Still, something left Anne when Sara left.

"I think that one day he'll invite me to his apartment along with other students to have dinner," Sara goes on. "I pretend to be sick and he takes me to his bedroom and I lie down. He puts his hand on my head to see if I have a fever. When he touches me I tell him I'm not sick at all."

"What does he say?"

"He says he understands. That we'll have to wait until the other students go home. He'll tell them he's going to take me to the infirmary himself."

"What happens next?" says Anne.

"Sometimes I imagine one thing," says Sara. "Sometimes other things. Before I go to sleep at night is when I imagine being with him."

"Do you make love?"

"Yes," says Sara.

"Does he talk to you afterwards?"

"Yes," says Sara.

"What about?"

"I haven't imagined that yet," says Sara. "But I will. After the first time we make love I ask him if we can make love again, and he says yes. Don't you imagine what it is like to make love to men?"

Anne does not. Anne does not answer. The two sit for a moment. Then Anne asks Sara if she imagines what she will do with her life. With her life after she graduates.

"I want to go to Paris and be a boulevardier," Sara says.

"With Professor Gassatt?" asks Anne. She doesn't know what Sara means.

"Oh no," says Sara. "Just because we make love doesn't mean I'm going to marry him. I'm not going to marry anyone. When I am in Paris I want to be by myself and sit in the cafés and imagine the apple trees. Just like in the song."

"What song?"

"'When the World Was Young.' Don't you know it? Do the apple trees still blossom in the breeze? When the world was young. My parents play it on their Hi-Fi all the time."

"I've never heard it," says Anne.

"What do you imagine you will do?" says Sara to Anne.

"Marry Professor Gassatt," she says. And laughs. "If you don't want him."

The Heart of Montaigne

"I understand you're a painter," Fredericka says.

"Yes."

"A good one, I understand."

"Thank you," she says. "Roy said you skin animals. That can't be true."

"It is not," she says. "In the winter I buy skins from trappers. I have a route I make with my truck through Western Kansas, Eastern Colorado and Southwestern Nebraska and I buy pelts. Then I sell them to a dealer in Kansas City. It's a business and I get material for my stories. I'm a writer of stories."

"Should I know your name?" Anne asks.

"No," Fredericka says. "I use a man's name. I write wildlife stories for men's outdoor magazines. I'm Fred Whitebread when I'm a man. They think I'm part Sioux." She thumps her chest. Anne laughs.

"I'm not sure I believe you," Anne says.

"I also write stories about France," Fredericka says.

"Not for men's magazines," Anne says.

"No," she says. "More for myself. Myself and the tax man. And the few literary magazines that will publish them."

"The tax man?" Anne says.

"If I write a story about France I can deduct my trip here. My politics aside, I'm compos mentis enough to know I live in a capitalist country. Do you do that with your paintings?"

"I don't know how to," she says.

"Look into it," Fredericka says. "You probably have more to gain than I do."

"I'll ask Roy," Anne says.

"Do it yourself," Fredericka says. There is a pause between them.

"Are your stories about France true or fiction?" Anne asks.

"They're fiction. But then so are the ones I write for outdoor magazines. Fred Whitebread and I just don't tell the male editors."

"I see," says Anne. "Where are you going when you leave Paris?"

"I always make a pilgrimage to Montaigne's heart," she says. "It's buried in a church not far from where Jane lives in the summer. His body is elsewhere. Do you know Montaigne?"

"No. Only the name. I think from college."

"He was a very great writer," says Fredericka. "He asked the right question."

"His heart is in a church?" says Anne.

"Yes," says Fredericka. "Buried in the floor in the church in Saint-Michel-de-Montaigne. I stand in the church with the swallows and talk to him. We have a heart-to-heart." She smiles.

"That's terrible," says Anne. They both laugh.

Anne, Is That You?

The death of Bird Four set her free in some way she could not— even later that summer when she was in Paris by herself and thought about it—fully understand. And that sense of freedom had come upon her immediately: Upon looking into the cage and seeing the bird dead on its side, small gnats on its eyes. He's dead, she said out loud, although no one was in the house. She took it to the sink and ground it down the garbage disposal.

Nothing else had had quite the same effect. Not when the children went away to college. Not when they emptied their rooms to get married. Not when she walked out on Roy five years ago after her clichéd jealousy had gotten the best of her and she moved into the small furnished apartment she had rented months before and kept all summer long until finally she packed herself up one Sunday while he was fishing at the lake (or humping Tina) and left. Not when she "spilled her guts" (Roy's phrase) that night in the apartment in Paris.

"Mother?"

"Anne? Is that you?"

"Yes."

"What's wrong? You don't call unless something's wrong."

"The fucking bird died."

"Don't swear, Anne. Your father didn't raise you to swear. Maybe it was the radon."

"It died on the back porch."

"Maybe there's radon on the back porch."

"No, mother. It just died."

"I'll get you another one."

"Please don't."

"I'll bring it over this afternoon."

"I'll kill it myself if you do."

"Anne!"

Were lists premises? Were choices conclusions? Were topics shadows? What is left when restraint leaves?

It Is Two Days Later

"I'm going to Paris by myself," Anne said.

"What am I supposed to do? Water the plants for two months? Talk to your mother? It doesn't sound like fun to me. I might as well stay at work."

"There is always Tina," she said.

"I thought we were over that," he said.

"Are we?" she said.

"Is that what this is about?" he said.

"No," she said.

"Is it about Fredericka?" he said.

"Yes," she said. "No."

"Then what?" he said.

"I don't know," she said.

"Well, maybe you better know before: one, you start telling me you want to leave for two months, and two, you throw old horse turds in my face. That fucking bitch started all this last year. That's what I think." He walked out of the house and went somewhere.

What Did She Know?

Could she use the apartment without Roy? What would she say to Fredericka if they met again? Would she be pleased? What about money? What would her mother say? Why was Montaigne's heart not buried with his body? Would Roy be at home when she got back? What would happen to her if he were not? Should she go back? Could she talk to Fredericka about that? What difference would it make if she didn't paint cheeses on tables with wine titled in French? Do people with fewer choices live better lives? What would the children say? Would her French continue to improve? Would Roy go back to Tina? Why did the faces in Uccello's painting seem childlike? And where did he get that red? Would she go to the restaurants Roy had scouted? Why had Fredericka said what she said that night in Paris? Would she find Sara Johnson in a café? What would she do about the painting that was growing somewhere in her body like a light: She is baby faced in red on horseback riding away from a crowd of mothers and husbands and yellow birds toward the front of the canvas and onto the Île de la Cité. Is Professor Gassett still a premise somewhere: his black hair and his green eyes the same as when the world was young? What was the right question? What did she know?

Barrel Heat

"That's a fine old trap gun you've got there. Nobody shoots those anymore, do they, Al?"

"They don't," I say.

"Not that you shoot anything new."

"I don't."

The man holding the gun—a trap-grade Winchester Model 12 with detailed engraving on the receiver, a ventilated rib running along the barrel, and a hand-checkered stock and forearm—is new to our club. In fact, this is his first time. I have been a member for twenty years. I am called The Champ. Ted, who has been doing the talking, is the President.

"My mother gave it to me when I was eighteen," the man says. "'A gift from your father long gone,' she'd say."

"There's a story for you, Al," says Ted.

"I thought so as well," says the man. "But my mother wouldn't tell me. 'Never mind,' was all I could get out of her."

The new man is sitting on a bench that faces the trap house and the five lanes that mark where the shooters stand. I am sitting beside him. Ted is standing in front of us. We have an hour or so of daylight for the shoot. It is my habit to shoot in the first squad, then go home. But I am late and so in the second squad. As it is summer and pleasant, the shoot might go into the evening with the lights on and the bright-white targets flying out into the dark of night if they don't get shot— "dropped," is the word for a missed target.

When I arrived I saw by the sign-up sheet that the man sitting next to me had put his name on position number three; that's where I usually start, and because I have been around so long, everybody lets me have it. Not that it makes much difference; I shoot well no matter where I begin. This evening I am number four.

But there is something more about the man sitting next to me other than he has taken my place: The trap gun he has, the Winchester Model 12 with hand checkered stock and forearm and the engravings on the receiver, that gun is my gun. I know the story. I know about the engravings. I knew his mother. I recognized his last name: Kincade.

When I was a university student I worked for a sporting goods store that had an engine repair and gunsmith shop in back. The gunsmith took a liking to me, and between my work on lawn mowers, taught me about guns and trap. His name was Bob Kincade and he had once been a champion shooter. But at some point he started to flinch just before he shot, and in this way dropped the target. Even a release trigger didn't help. After that he was no longer competitive, and you could see him at various trap clubs in the area sitting in his truck, not even getting out to say hello to the men against whom he had once shot. Sometime during the shoot he'd drive away. It was in those days that I knew him.

One Friday he asked if I might like to shoot a round of trap at the local club.

"I don't have a gun," I said.

"Use one of mine," he said. "Tomorrow evening. Seven. Before the sun goes down. I bring shells. You bring dollar for shoot."

"Where?" I said. He told me how to get to the club.

No one knew much about Bob Kincade: where he lived, how he became a champion trap shooter, where he came from. Only that he lived alone with a daughter about my age—or so

Mr. Wilson, the store's owner, told me. To look at Bob Kincade people guessed he had tribal blood: Sioux. Cherokee. Navajo. Shoshone. It was in his face and the way he talked. Nobody asked. He was a tall man with large, rough hands. My guess is he might have been sixty.

What everyone did know about Bob Kincade was that he was an excellent gunsmith who took great care, not only in repairing the guns brought to him, but in refinishing them with finely tooled checkering on the forearms and stocks. And with delicate engravings on the receivers: not of flying ducks or pheasants or pointing dogs as you might expect, but from drawings that he'd bring to work—drawings on a single sheet of heavy paper with a ruled line down the middle and a small *R* at the top of one side, and a small *L* on the top of the other: faces, flowers, tree branches, horse heads, moons, letters—all repeated with variations on each side of the receiver so that the repetition formed a design of its own, the letters becoming a word or a name if you looked carefully enough, or through the large mounted magnifying glass on Bob Kincade's bench that he used to make the engravings. And the designs were in a hand not his because I knew his coarse script from the receipts he'd write for the guns he was to repair. Before the summer was over, I'd learn whose hand it was.

"Don't wear ball cap. Don't sight down barrel. Keep both eyes open," he said to me when I got to the trap club. He was sitting in his truck, a sagging short bed of an old Dodge. The window was down. I saw that some of the men were looking our way. I learned later this was Kincade's home trap club and so they knew him, and knew what had happened that he didn't shoot anymore. None of them came up.

"Here," he said, and through the open window passed me a shotgun and a box of shells. "You shoot second squad. Sign for number three. Shoot quick. Choose your call. Stay with it.

You got dollar?" I said I did. And then, even though it was summer and the cool of the evening was not yet coming on, he rolled up the window and stared straight ahead. I wondered what he meant by choosing my call.

Looking back on it, I don't know what made Bob Kincade think I might be a good shot. True, I was on the university baseball team and its best hitter, so I had something of an eye. Once in a while, I'd take a gun from the rack near his bench and put it to my shoulder, but that was about it. I didn't come from a hunting family, much less a trap-shooting one. Maybe he saw in me something he wanted to see and that I didn't. That happens.

"Use 'yo' for your call," said the man who kept score. "It was his, and he'll be pleased."

Most of the men said "pull" when they wanted the target, although one man grunted. Two or three of them shot quickly and the target was "smoked"—as the men called it when there were no chunks flying off. Two others dropped five or six targets. The man who grunted for his call shot twenty-five of twenty-five, all of them quickly, all of them smoked.

I missed the first target out, then broke three in a row, but not quickly or smoked. Then I missed the last one. From position four, I missed the first two, broke the last three, the final one quickly and smoked. Then I broke every target after that, some of them quickly and smoked, but not all of them until the final five, which I broke quickly—and all them were smoked. The man who told me to choose "yo" shook my hand as we came away from the line. When I looked, Bob Kincade was driving away.

Monday he was not at work. Nor the rest of the week. I had brought his gun to the shop and cleaned it. It was a Winchester Model 12 trap grade with a plain receiver and factory checkering on the forearm and stock. Ventilated rib running the length of the barrel. Sometimes I would put it to my shoulder and take aim at the pigeons flying up and down the alley that you could see out the back of the shop when the large work door was open. Once I said yo! and Mr. Wilson smiled. When I asked him where Bob Kincade had gone, he said out of town on a bus to watch a few shoots. His truck was too old for long trips down memory lane.

The following Saturday, I bought a box of shells and went back to the gun club with Bob Kincade's gun and a dollar. He was there, but did not look at me, nor roll down his window. I thought to go over and ask him if it was all right to use his gun again, but his straight-ahead stare stopped me. I shot in the first squad, broke twenty-five, all quickly, and all smoked. When I came off the line I could see his truck leaving. The following Monday, he was back at work.

You shoot trap from sixteen yards up to twenty-seven yards, each yard numbered on the five lanes running at angles toward the trap house so that, seen from above, the arrangement looks like a fan with the trap-house square sixteen yards from the fan's base. At the trap club where I first shot, that fan was called "the infield." Where the targets sailed was called "the outfield." That is also true where I now shoot.

When there is a "registered" shoot, the kind of competition where men like Bob Kincade participate, the better shot must shoot from greater distances. That first and second night at Bob Kincade's club we all shot from sixteen yards. In competition Bob Kincade always shot from twenty-seven yards, and still he beat men who shot from shorter distances. If you have no "registered" targets, you shoot from sixteen yards until you get your "number." By my memory in those days you had to shoot a thousand such targets, usually at rounds of fifty-to-a-hundred— that is, two to four squad's worth.

The reason I was good at it was because it was like hitting a baseball, only in reverse: the ball going away from home plate of the trap house instead of toward it, but still there it was: high and fast off the corner of the plate one time, down the middle another time, then on the other corner. You never knew where the pitcher might throw the ball or the trap might throw the target. My gun was my bat; I kept both eyes open and on the ball.

"Not for twenty years," says the man sitting next to me. Ted had asked him when he last shot trap.

"My mother drove me around to the local trap clubs where my father shot and I shot a round at each for the memory of who he was. I was pretty good at it. Some of the men he shot against were still alive and they talked about him."

"Your father was a trap shooter?" Ted asks.

"Among the best. There were trophies around the house. And a rack of guns he had used. But I didn't take to it, and when my mother died, I sold the guns—all except this one because it has one of her drawings for the engravings."

He turns the Model 12 over so we see both sides of the receiver. The design is one of repeated letters and lips and hands, eyes—not that you could tell that. It seemed more like scrollwork: delicate and mysterious. My name is portioned out like code. And another's as well.

"You don't see that on most guns," Ted says. "Do you, Al?"

"You don't," I say.

"One gun and one drawing were missing," the man says. "I know because my father engraved his receivers from designs by my mother. Then he would make frames for the drawings. They were hanging on the walls when I was growing up. The drawing for this gun was missing. And there was a drawing for a gun we didn't have. A missing drawing, a missing gun. My mother wouldn't tell me about either. Only, 'never mind.'"

"Do you have the other drawings?" I ask.

"Yes. I took them when I cleaned out the house."

"Show him your gun," Ted says. "His has engravings as well. Sort of like yours."

"Later," I say. My gun is in the clubhouse.

When Bob Kincade came into the shop the Monday morning after I had borrowed his gun he did not talk to me and I sensed he did not want me to talk to him. I had again cleaned the gun and laid it out on the bench. He opened the action and looked down the barrel to see if I had cleaned that as well: I had. Then he put it aside. We worked together in silence, me cleaning carburetors, he hand-checkering stocks.

For lunch he usually brought a brown bag; I took mine across the street at the Tee-Pee Tavern because of a waitress who had been a student with me in my writing class.

"I have extra from home," he said as I was about to leave. "Pop for you."

I joined him at his bench by pulling up a stool. The sandwiches were made of thick, dark-brown bread and filled with sliced tomatoes, lettuce, onions and cheese. I drank the pop. Bob Kincade drank tea from a large Mason jar.

"Lisa," he said, as he unwrapped the sandwiches from the wax paper. "From her baking and the garden she tends," referring, I supposed, to his daughter and to the bread as well as the tomatoes and onions and lettuce. "Sun tea," he said, as he drank his tea from the jar, not pouring it into a cup or glass. "Lisa."

At the end of lunch he folded the wax paper into the brown paper bag, swept off the crumbs from his work bench, took a final drink of tea, and said:

"When we close today, I want to talk to you." Yes, I said.

Betting on trap shooters is called a Calcutta and is illegal. The shooter is "The Mark"— or was where I shot. Bob Kincade had once been a Mark, but when he began gambling on me he would become The Man. Sometimes two Marks are being bet against one another, like a two-man horse race. Not that either one would know it. This is what Bob Kincade wanted to talk about.

"And don't bring girlfriends," he said. "No women in trap clubs. Sometimes in the trucks watching." He gave me directions to the trap club where I was to shoot and handed me the gun I had used the week before. "Don't come to me afterwards." Yes, I said. "Don't break all. Don't smoke all you break." Yes, I said.

In this way I began shooting The Calcutta at the trap clubs of small towns in the area: Eudora, Vinland, Overbrook, Perry, Lecompton, Pleasant Grove, Berryton, and once as far south as Centropolis. All of them clubs where Bob Kindcade was known as a great trap shooter and afterwards could be seen sitting in his truck watching what he could no longer do—in this case, on that first Saturday at the trap club just outside of Lone Star, me shooting from the middle position at sixteen yards and calling yo! when I wanted the target, dropping three, with only a dozen or so smoked. If he had bet, The Man would have lost money on his Mark.

"Al used to be a champion," Ted says to the man sitting next to me. "Isn't that right, Al."

The first squad is at the line. Something is not right with the trap and so the men stand there, the muzzles of their guns resting on small pads at each position.

"You were?" By my guess he is forty plus to my sixty plus.

"It might have been true once, but it didn't work out."

"He still smokes them," says Ted. "Not always twenty-five, but sometimes." There is a pause among us while we listen to the men fixing the trap. Ted asks if he is needed. He is not.

"You from around here?" Ted says to Kincade.

"Visiting," he says. "My son just took a job at the college. This is his gun now but he doesn't have any interest. He's the one who told me how to get here." We are quiet for a moment. More than a pause.

"Tell us the story about your old gun," Ted says to me; he is prodding. My "old gun" is a Parker single-barrel trap gun, engraved and hand-checkered. It is even older than Kincade's Winchester Model 12. And it is not my gun. Nor have I told anyone its story.

"I pay you half what you win, plus gun when it's over," Bob Kincade said to me the Monday after the Lone Star shoot. I asked him why it would be over.

"Something get you," he said. "Maybe they figure it out. I won't be there every time. Lisa, she come. Don't talk to her either. Don't smoke them unless you see my hand or hers on the top of steering wheel. Otherwise, drop two or three. When you see we leave, quit." Yes, I said.

He told me we'd keep the gun on the rack near his bench and that I should clean it each time I used it. He said he would get new wood for the stock and forearm from some town in Missouri. He said nothing about the receiver. I wondered if the "something that would get me" would be flinching. But it was not.

It took two more Saturdays before I saw Kincade's hand at the top of the steering wheel, and then I smoked them all, hitting twenty-five in the first squad, and then twenty-five in the second. As I was walking off the line I saw him collect his bets and then start the truck. I said "no," when asked if I wanted to sign up for the third squad as there was a slot left.

At clubs when Kincade's hand was not at the top of the steering wheel, the next Monday when I'd clean the gun there was no money. But when I smoked them all on a Saturday or Sunday, the following Monday there was money on his work bench, stacked but not divided until we had lunch together, and then Bob Kincade would sort the bills into two equal piles as he shared his sandwiches. When he saw I was not finishing my pop, he brought an extra Mason jar of tea. "Lisa," he said. "Sun tea."

One Saturday at Pleasant Grove, he was not there but Lisa was, sitting in the truck as men came up to her at the open window. After a moment she'd put out her palm for a pat of a handshake. She was about my age: black hair, thin lipped, large deep green eyes, delicate hands—one of which was on the top of the steering wheel. Around her neck, which was long and pale, she wore a red kerchief. If there was tribal blood in her it did not show. Going back and forth between the club's bench and my car, I'd pass the truck and look. Once she smiled. There was nothing about her beauty that would make you think she was Bob Kincade's daughter.

I shot twenty-five, but did not smoke them all. When I turned around, she was still there, her hand on the steering wheel. I broke the next twenty-five, smoking them all. When I came off the line, she was driving away. I saw her eyes looking at me in the rearview mirror.

I lived in a small apartment across the street from the sporting goods store and above the Tee-Pee Tavern, and sometimes, after closing, the waitress that was in my writing class would come up the stairs from the parking lot behind the tavern with a six-pack of Coors and spend the night. She had a boyfriend who had gone home to St. Louis for the summer and once in a while she'd meet him there.

We knew we were not in love, but we were something to one another and that felt good as well. Later, she wrote a fine erotic story about us that got published. The story was called "Barrel Heat," and its title came from what finally "got me" at trap shooting. However, her story was not about trap shooting, but about being my lover that summer while not being in love with me and discovering that she was not in love with her St. Louis boyfriend either—but not in love in a different way. *No two ways of not being in love with your lover are the same,* was the first sentence of the story. It was a sentence I wish I had written, as was the story that followed.

Monday evening after the shoot at Pleasant Grove, I was having a beer at the Tee-Pee Tavern and my waitress girlfriend was not there. But Lisa was. Bob Kincade had not been at work that day and Mr. Wilson said he had taken the bus to Missouri to get stocks and forearms.

Lisa was sitting by herself on a barstool. I had come in the back door from the parking lot after having made myself dinner. Lisa was wearing the same red kerchief around her neck, blue jeans, and a summer, yellow blouse with pearl-like buttons and a red collar. Her legs were long. She turned when I came in, smiled, and patted the empty stool beside her. I sat down and ordered a draw.

"You are a very fine shot," she said. This was after a moment of silence between us because I did not know what to say other than "hello" and found myself looking at her reflection in the mirror behind the bar. "Bob has told me this, and it is true."

"And you make very good sun tea," I said as I turned to look at her. "And grow a garden, I understand."

"Yes," she said. There was a moment of silence. More than a pause. I looked at her in the mirror.

"I understand your father has gone to buy gun stocks and forearms," I said.

"What?" she said.

"I understand that . . . " but I did not finish the sentence because she pushed her half-finished beer away, turned on her stool, got off, and walked out of the mirror behind the bar and through the front door.

The trap has been fixed and Mr. Kincade and I are now sitting by ourselves because Ted has gone to push the button that throws the targets. He also has a clipboard on which he'll mark the hits and dropped; under normal circumstances I would have gotten a folding chair from the clubhouse and done that chore for him.

"Was your father Bob Kincade?" I ask.

"Why, yes."

"I went to school in Lawrence," I say before he can ask how I knew. "I worked at Wilson Sporting Goods store when he did."

"Did you shoot with my father?"

"I did not."

The first squad is starting. There is no one among them smoking targets; no one will break twenty-five. The reason I am called the Champ is because I am graded on the curve. I give my writing students the same consideration.

The next Monday morning Bob Kincade was at work. He had stocks and forearms on his bench. From a sink he'd wet a shop rag and wipe down a stock, then run his hand over it, then wet it again. When he'd do that the grain would show, and in this way—as he told me at lunch—he knew the quality of the wood and how to checker it. For the gun I was using, he had picked a burled walnut. That afternoon he began to checker the stock. By the following Saturday, both the stock and the forearm were done. The engraving, he said, would come later. "Lisa," he said.

It was Mr. Wilson who one day showed me the gun Bob Kincade had used to shoot trap: a single barrel Parker. Hand-checkered stock and forearm. Engravings on the receiver and up along the lower part of the barrel where the chamber was. A matted rib. He had used others over the years, Mr. Wilson told me, but this one was special: he had won many championships with it, including a national one in Ohio.

Bob Kincade kept the Parker in the store's safe where other rare and expensive guns for sale were kept: Purdeys, Pigeon Grade Model 12s, Winchester Model 21s. Over and Under Broadway Ribbed Brownings. And Bob Kincade's trap grade single-barrel Parker into which he had put a release trigger (you don't "pull" it, you pull it back before you shoot, then "release" it, and that fires the gun) in order to fool his reflexes. Mr. Wilson told me that when that did not work, Kincade took out the trigger, reinstalled the original, cleaned the gun, then put it in the safe and never used it again. Not to be able to shoot well had smoked something inside Bob Kincade. And even with no son to pass it to, Mr. Wilson told me, the Parker was not for sale.

"Great invention, ventilated ribs," said the man who grunted his call that first time I shot. We were walking out to the line at Eudora.

"I guess," I said.

He had shot with me a few times since then. His number was twenty-four, and from there he breaks that number more often than not. Sometimes more. A few times less. He was Bob Kincade's age. Like me, I suspected he was a Mark, but to whom I did not know.

"When we only had matted ribs or plain barrels you saw the heat waves coming off," he said. "Now you only see them if you look for them."

Lisa was there. Her hand was on the steering wheel. She had raised it once as if to say hello. Or at least that was what I liked to think.

"What about heat waves?" I said.

"They distort the target if you look through them," the man said. "Like water will distort a catfish if you shoot him in a creek. You shoot catfish?"

"No," I said.

"You got to aim above them in water," the man said as I walked to the sixteen yard line while he stayed at twenty-four. "'Barrel heat' is what we used to call it," he said. "It's not what got Bob Kincade; that was the flinch. Not even a release trigger helped. I think you know about Bob Kincade?"

"Yes," I said.

I dropped one in the first squad and two in the second. Coming off the second round, I saw Lisa pay out in bills from a roll. The following Monday Bob Kincade was at work but did not talk to me and did not bring me lunch. I went over to the Teepee and then again that night for a meal and more than a few beers. Later, my girlfriend not in love with me came into the apartment and spent the night. The next morning she left for St. Louis. Bob Kincade was not at work again until Friday, just before I was to shoot at Vinland. Wednesday, Lisa was at the Teepee in a booth by the back door.

"Where has your father gone?"

"You did not shoot so well at Eudora," she said instead of answering my question. "We bet on you at twenty-five each time. Twenty-four and bets are off. Less than twenty-four, we pay. I don't want you to be long gone as a Mark." Her eyes were fixed on me.

"Is that why your father is not at work?"

"He has taken a bus to Norton to watch the state championship." She seemed about to say something more, but did not. With no mirror we looked directly at one another. Her face that night even now I cannot forget.

One day I stayed late at the store. There were lawn mower blades to sharpen before the next morning. I had a key to lock up. Going through the store to the front door I noticed that Mr. Wilson had not locked the gun safe and I went over to do so. Inside was the Parker and I took it out.

On the receiver was the same kind of design I had seen on other guns Bob Kincade had engraved, only more elaborate and more difficult to decipher: feathers, letters, hands, eyes, and what appeared to be fragments of the gun itself. Moving from the receiver onto the chamber of the barrel the design seemed to tell a story, the ending of which was a ceremony of some sort that could be read only by turning the gun over, so that what began on the top of the barrel was continued in a circle to the sides and bottom: multiple hands, eyes, lips, Ls and Bs and Ks scattered about—all in delicate etching. It must be true, I thought, looking at Bob Kincade's gun, that he was indeed tribal, and what Lisa had depicted was a ceremony of that fact.

I put the gun in the safe and locked it. Halfway across the street I understood the story on the gun. And what it meant to have something inside you smoked. In the booth by the back door was Lisa.

The second squad is getting up to shoot. Mr. Kincade turns to me.

"Would you like to shoot my gun?" he says. "In memory of my father since you knew him. I don't mind watching. One champ shooting another champ's gun. Someone can take my place."

"How about we shoot together?"

"O.K.," he says and seems pleased I have asked. He stuffs his pockets with shells and walks toward the line. I go into the clubhouse to get his father's Parker and my shell pouch. I am shooting number four, next to him. We are all at sixteen yards. His call is yo! And he breaks the first target out—not smoking it—but solid. I smoke mine and he smiles, for both my yo! I think, and the quick-smoked target. In this way we begin.

One Monday after I shot poorly, Bob Kincade tied a small piece of red cloth to the end of the Model 12.

"It will keep you from looking at barrel heat," he said.

In recent shoots I had been breaking twenty-five as before, but sometimes not quickly and not always smoked. Apparently he knew the trouble. "Lisa's," he said about the cloth. "From old kerchief like she wears." Then after a moment he said: "He is good, not as good as I was. He knows you are my Mark."

The next week, with Lisa in the truck, I broke twenty-five three times, all of them smoked. Still, there was the barrel heat. It was like looking for a curve ball that doesn't come and then the fastball gets you.

The following Monday, Bob Kincade was not at work. That night in bed I heard the back door to my apartment open and thought it was my waitress lover, but remembered she was to be in St. Louis. It was Lisa. Her step was soft, as she did not know where to find me. Then she did.

The next Friday the drawing for the Model 12 was on Bob Kincade's bench.

"For the gun," he said. "Lisa." Yes, I said.

From then on I shot better and worse, and there were times when I lost money for them and times I won money. And whenever Bob Kincade was away to get wood, or at other trap shoots out of town where he would watch old friends shoot, Lisa would be with me, coming up the back stairs, and only once did she meet my waitress lover, Lisa coming down the stairs as the waitress was going up—and it was the waitress who told me about it, and how she did not continue up the stairs that night and wanted me to know she was not angry, but only sad. Some of this she included in her own story and I have wondered all these years if Lisa ever read that story because the magazine that published it put copies around town and at the university. It was my waitress lover who asked me if I knew that Lisa was Bob Kincade's wife.

By September, barrel heat was getting to me. I could see it coming off the rib as I shot. While others were shooting, I would look down the barrel and there it was. Not even Lisa's kerchief helped. There were days when I shot twenty-two, but there were still days when I shot twenty-five, but not all of them smoked. Nights with Lisa we would not talk about it. The beauty of her eyes in the dark seemed lit from behind; her hands and neck were the beauty of her entire body, and the memory of her from the night before repeated itself the next day as if it were multiple engravings. The more we were together, the more difficult it was for me to shoot—or to be at work with Bob Kincade. No love for Lisa is like any other love.

"We will stop after next Saturday," Bob Kincade said to me one Monday. There was money on the workbench, as was the gun. Lunch, too. For both of us. Sun tea. And at the end of the bench a small drawing. I went over to look at it.

"I will make an engraving this week," he said. "Then the gun is yours. Wilson says you are quitting to go back to school." Yes, I said. I looked at the drawing: delicate, intricate and, like the others, with a line down the middle for right and left on the receiver. There was no obvious story, but not all stories are obvious. There was more than a pause between us.

"I know about you and Lisa," he said. I said nothing. "Lisa," he said as he put our lunch on the workbench. "Lisa," he said as he gave me my Mason jar of sun tea. *Lisa*, I said myself, saying nothing else to Bob Kincade the rest of the day—or, as it turned out, the rest of his life. "And you being a boy to me," were the last words Bob Kincade ever said to me.

Mr. Kincade and I are shooting well. He is breaking targets, sometimes even smoking them. I am smoking mine. There is barrel heat coming off the Parker but I am shooting through it with both eyes wide open and the memory of a bit of red handkerchief at the muzzle's end. The targets are fastballs on one corner of the plate or the other—or down the middle. As I have started at number four, I am now finishing where I usually begin. The end of the game is now five targets away.

"Ready?" I say.

"Yo!" he says, and he smokes number twenty-one, as do I.

It is September. My gun was, as promised, engraved the week after my final shoot. There is money. Bob Kincade is not there; Mr. Wilson got the gun and the money from the safe. He thanked me for my summer's work and hoped I'd return next summer.

Walking across the street, I go into the Teepee and sit in the booth at the back near the door and lay the gun on the table.

I order a draw and study the engravings. My lover waitress comes in for her shift, but before it starts, she pulls herself a beer and joins me. It is from her that I get the drawing of the engravings on my gun. "Lisa," is what she says when she hands it to me, saying as well that they knew each other in high school. There is a pause between us as I study the drawing. Then my waitress lover makes a motion with her hand to turn it over. On the other side there is this: *I can never see you again. You must not try to find me or ask for me or ask why. One day I might want your gun. It will be a trade.* All written in a script like the ones for her designs, and like those designs, there seemed something to be deciphered. My waitress lover says she does not understand what any of this means. Nor do I.

Fall contracts into winter. Bob Kincade dies. Lisa is not to be found. That spring, playing shortstop for the university team, I don't hit very well. In the summer I go back to work at Wilson's. Bob Kincade's bench is as he left it. Mr. Wilson tells me that Lisa took the Parker. Then one day walking across the street to the Teepee, I see an old Dodge truck heading out of town. When I get to my apartment, the Model 12 is gone, but the Parker is there with a one-word note: *Lisa.* Written in the script of the engravings, this time with a drawing around her name that tells a story I cannot read.

Twenty-two, smoked by two yo!s. Twenty-three. Twenty-four. Pause. Yo! Twenty-five. Yo! Twenty-five. We are two champs at sixteen yards and all smiles and hand shakes.

"Take it," Mr. Kincade says as he hands me my Model 12. "My son has no interest."

"Then take the Parker," I say. We are back at the bench. "That's your mother and father getting married in the engraving. It's the missing gun." He is looking at the Parker, turning it over on his lap. There is more than a moment's silence.

"I thought they were never married," he says. The third squad is going to the line.

"What?" I say.

"I thought he died just before they were to be married. And just before I was born. That's what I thought my mother meant when she'd say 'he's long gone.'"

He is looking at the Parker as if trying to find the truth of the past. In the infield the third shoot is starting. It occurs to me I have not asked how his mother died. Or if she died. *Lisa*, I say to myself—or think I do, but he looks up and, as if he has he heard me, says:

"She died this year. She was to come with me to see my son take up his job. She . . . " But before he can go on I ask:

"What's your son's job at the college?

"Baseball coach. He's the new baseball coach."

The Billion-Dollar Dream

Arlene Had Left Him a Year Ago

Paul Andrews began putting himself to sleep by fantasizing he had a Billion dollars. Not a million dollars. A Billion. (He always capitalized Billion.) Each night Paul would add more layers to his story: the money had come from a mysterious source who would never reveal himself (or "herself," as Paul rewrote a few nights into his dream). Then, the money could only be used in specified ways. Next, the method of spending the money had to be worked out: Credit cards (without limits)? Checks? Letters of credit? Bank transfers? Cash in suitcases? The stuff of movies and novels. In this way the plot and the characters and settings and the money itself (because it was earning interest) accumulated. At work Paul looked forward to going to sleep.

Arlene had left him a year ago. Their three children were in California.

Lilly Was in Charge of Ordering

The house was too big for Paul. That's what everybody said. "Everybody" was his sister-in-law Janet and Lilly Frame, the small blond assistant manager of Books-and-Joe-to-Go, the bookstore-cum-coffeehouse that Paul owned with Janet and his older brother Lloyd.

"If you live in spaces too big for your 'essence,'" Lilly Frame said, "you cannot be at 'one' with yourself. That is why Marie Antoinette went from the Palace at Versailles to the Petit Trianon. Versailles was too big for her 'essence,' and one assumes she had a very big 'essence,' considering who she was." Lilly smiled, as she usually did after one of her "monos," as she called them. But Paul could never tell if Lilly's smile was amusement at herself or not.

"If you are not contained by yourself, you begin to ooze out of yourself," Lilly continued. "A glass may be half full or half empty. That is not the point. The point is that it is a glass, and it confines water, and the water does not ooze out of itself. If you are everywhere, you are nowhere. And don't tell me about lakes and rain and seas. That's something else." Again, Lilly smiled.

The house in question was a "rancher" that he and Arlene had agreed upon after the birth of their second child. They ordered the plans from a magazine, and the builder put in a few suggestions—but nothing made the house exceptional in either its floor plan or its exterior. It was a long single story with a lot of lawn to mow and a patio for summer cooking. No pool.

There were, however, the two sets of washers and dryers that everybody thought rather ingenious. One set was located in an alcove between the kitchen and the garage, and the second set was located in the hallway at the other end of the house that joined the bedrooms. In this way Arlene could wash the sheets and the children's clothes without lugging the laundry very far, and she could wash the tablecloths and napkins at the other end where Paul could also wash his work clothes—as long as he wiped out the tub afterwards.

"Very well conceived," is what Janet said at the time. She had just gotten her real-estate license. "Very well conceived." Later, after Arlene left, Janet said to Paul: "What will you do with two sets of washers and dryers? The place has curb appeal. You can get a bundle for it. I'll sell it for half the fee."

"Leave him alone," said Lloyd.

Open This Now

At nights Paul would restart his Billion-dollar dream from the beginning by getting notified of the money; then he would "speed dream" to where he had left off the night before. In an early version, a letter had come with Important or Open This Now or Timed Material stamped on it and Paul would have himself toss it in the waste basket. Later in the dream he'd get up in the night for a glass of milk and, seeing the crumpled Important in the trash, pick it out. In some versions he tears the letter as he opens it and has to piece it back together on the counter. Other nights, coffee grounds from the morning have blotted the letter, so that it is difficult to read. But in all versions is his Billion dollars—or at least the letter telling Paul whom to contact to get his Billion dollars, which was not yet the Billion dollars, but only a "large bequest."

After a few nights, Paul began to imagine the letter's text: *You do not know me, or my firm. But it is important that you contact me as soon as possible because we have a very large bequest that is yours.* Paul had the letter signed *Robert Day*, the name of an author who had recently been at Books-and-Joe-to-Go for a reading and book autographing. Later, Paul changed *very large* to *substantial.* To get this far had taken him the first week of what had been a wet April.

Even Now He Did Not Mention the Matter

Although Lilly Frame had for a number of years dated the sales manager of a local spice company, she had never married. She still "saw" her former lover now and then, but it was no longer "heavy duty-duty."

Lilly was "a bit in love" with Paul and had been from when she first came to work at the bookstore. She considered Paul handsome (he was not, by most standards—including his own); she liked the way Paul put his index fingers on either side of his brow when he was trying to concentrate; she thought the paperclip he used to fasten a broken hinge on his glasses endearing. She admired the way he took time to talk to the customers, including the ones who were probably not going to buy anything. He seemed interested in what people had to say—in what Lilly had to say—even though Lilly knew she could be "flaky" at times. When Lilly talked she would put finger quotes in the air around such phrases as "essence," and "monos" and "heavy duty-duty." Or (in her mind) "a bit in love." Then she would feel herself smile, as if that were part of the punctuation.

Lilly could not understand why Arlene had left Paul. But she was impressed that Paul had not said much about it, either about the divorce (which took everyone at the bookstore by surprise), or about what must have gone on before. Even now he did not mention the matter.

"Let me fix you dinner," Lilly said to Paul one afternoon. "You must be lonely with that big kitchen and those two sets of washers and dryers. I make decent paella with real saffron, and I'll put it together at my apartment and bring it ready to serve and I'll clean up afterwards. I'll even bring the wine. And flan for dessert. *A bueno?* With the question mark upside down?"

"How sweet of you," said Paul, and let it go at that.

Are You Paul Andrews?

During the second week of his Billion-dollar dream, Paul has the phone ring just as he gets home from work. It might be Janet inviting him to dinner. Or someone selling mortuary insurance. But at the ring just before his recording kicks in, he has himself pick it up. A woman says: *Are you Paul Andrews? Yes.* Then she says: *Just a moment,* and after a few clicks a man's voice introduces himself as Robert Day and says that he represents a client who has a substantial bequest to make to a Mr. Paul David Andrews of 2634 Midi Lane. *Are you that Paul Andrews?*

I am.

Please come by my office tomorrow morning at ten?

I shall.

In the choice between the coffee-stained letter and the phone call, Paul settled on the phone call because he liked the woman's voice, a woman he named Bonita which, he knew from his college days, meant "pretty" in Spanish. It was also a small "tuna," Lilly had told him.

"I can cook that for you instead of the paella," she had said.

Janet Decided to Find Paul a Lover

Janet was also attracted to Paul, and had been from their college days. "Enamored," she now called it to herself. She liked Paul for pretty much the same reasons Lilly did, although it was also true that she had never liked Arlene and thought Paul deserved better. Janet was glad Arlene was history. Out of the picture. On the coast. Toast.

Janet decided to find Paul a lover. It didn't make much difference if the woman was married or not. Some of her friends had had affairs in recent years: none of them had been caught; all of them confided to Janet that they were happy to have had such men in their lives; all of them had told her they had become better wives ("person" was what one of her friends had said) because of the affairs. None of them rattled on about how they hated to live a lie, or that they felt "cheated" not to have a husband as kind and as understanding a man as was their lover; or that their husband deserved this infidelity because of whatever "poking around" he was probably doing. Nor did any of these women tell Janet they wanted to leave their husbands for their lovers. Janet prided herself on being the kind of woman other women could talk to. She kept their secrets. She had kept one about Paul all these years. Among the women Janet considered for Paul, she settled on Lilly Frame.

"I Love Men Who Take Their Coffee Black"

Paul arrives at Robert Day's office on the top floor of an elegant steel and glass building in nearby Washington, D. C. at the appointed time. He is greeted by Bonita who is tall, has blond hair (blonder than Lilly's), brown eyes, a bright, wide smile, and a lovely figure. Fifteen years younger than Paul, she nonetheless looks at him as if struck by his presence. Perhaps it has to do with the Billion dollars he is about to get, but Paul decides not to make that so: Bonita will know nothing of it.

"Mr. Day will be with you in a moment," Bonita says as she escorts Paul into a large corner office with windows on two sides, a large desk in the middle (that has nothing on it but a cell phone), and a coffee table with two chairs and a couch. There are framed photographs on the wall. Some Paul notices are of writers too long dead to have been photographed. Dante, for one. But when Paul tries to change the photograph into an etching, it turns into a photograph of Shakespeare. Then one of Dr. Johnson. There is also a glass case filled with autographed baseballs.

" My name is Bonita," Paul has Bonita say after a moment. "It means 'pretty' in Spanish. Not that I am Spanish. But my mother majored in Spanish and liked the name. May I get you a cup of coffee?"

"Yes," says Paul.

"Cream or sugar?" says Bonita. "Both?"

"Black."

"I love men who take their coffee black."

"Aren't you answering your phone messages these days?" It was Janet. She was standing in Paul's kitchen when he came in the back door. He knew she was there because of her white Lexus in the driveway.

"I forget to listen to them," he said.

"I need to know if I can pry you out of this big house with its two washers and dryers over to our big house for dinner on Saturday. I have someone I want you to meet."

"That's very sweet of you," Paul said.

"You can't just leave it at that," Janet said. "I need to know so I can invite her."

"I have someone in my life," said Paul.

"I don't believe you," said Janet. "What's her name?"

"Bonita," he said. "It means *tuna* in Spanish."

"*Tuna. Lobster.*" said Janet. "Be at our house for dinner Saturday at 6 P.M. And wear good glasses, not the ones with the paper clip. What woman can like that?"

"If you say so," said Paul.

It Was the Way Paul Traveled

In college Paul had been a geography major: steppes, tropics, latitudes and longitudes, lava plateaus, time zones, and (his favorite projection) plate carre. As he learned the physical organization of the planet, he had studied with equal pleasure its political divisions: countries, provinces, states, and cities. He had not only memorized the names of countries and regions current to his education (such as Ethiopia), but was delighted to learn that Ethiopia had once been Abyssinia, which in turn led him to a novel recommended by an English professor titled *The Prince of Abyssinia,* and from there to a travelogue by a Portuguese priest named Lobo. It was the way Paul traveled. Then and now.

Paul had no desire to visit the places whose names and provinces and regions and capitals and great cities he knew in literary ways: *From Stettin in the Baltic to Trieste in the Adriatic*, he used to say to see if anyone knew either the man who said it or the line across Europe that man had drawn in the mind's eye of his audience (and where was that audience?).

When the Soviet Union broke up, Paul was the only one among his friends who could name its constituent parts: from Litovskaja in the north (he preferred the traditional spellings) to Turkmenskaja in the south—just to use the western edge. And well before Yugoslavia broke apart, he could do a free hand diagram of all it states—and its one "duchy," a word he found amusing.

Paul's major professor had encouraged him to go to graduate school. But it was about this time he met Arlene, and she thought there was not much future in Paul becoming a geographer, whatever they did. Shortly after graduation (and marriage), Paul joined Lloyd and Janet in buying the bookstore. It had been a good decision: he liked the book business and he had made a good living at it, putting their children through college, and, of course, buying and maintaining his house. Nor did Arlene have to work.

"A Billion Dollars"

"We have some . . . well . . . astounding news for you Paul David Andrews," says Robert Day as he enters the office. Bonita has left. With a smile. A smile Paul makes different from Lilly Frame's smile. More knowing.

Robert Day takes a seat in one of the chairs by the coffee table. He glances around, gets up and goes to his desk, checks the cell phone, then returns bringing the phone with him. He looks just like the Robert Day who had recently read at Books-and-Joe-to-Go, and for a moment Paul forgot that was the name he had given him.

"We have a client who has made you a great gift."

"Yes."

"Our client wants you to share the fabulous wealth that our client's astute business sense has created. I must—as you probably notice—avoid even a pronoun. Nor can I tell you the nature of the business that generated the money. Even that you are getting the money must remain a secret. Only three of us know."

"I understand."

"Let us just say," continues Robert Day, "that our client wants you to have what will seem to you like an enormous sum of money, but which is to our client—while not insignificant—is not the greater share of the net worth."

"How much?"

"A Billion dollars." Robert Day looks at the cell phone because it is making a discrete ring. "Your benefactor on the line," he says.

Later that night, when Paul awoke and did not immediately go back to sleep, instead of Robert Day telling him he has a Billion dollars, he has Robert Day hand him a piece of paper. Paul reads it twice. Bonita comes in and Paul turns the paper upside down on the table. Paul notices Bonita's neck is exceptionally pretty. Bonita smiles. In her smile Paul senses she knows that he has created her, and this makes him uneasy, and he tries to drop the smile from the scene, but before he can, Bonita leaves.

Paul picks the second version of how he gets his Billion dollars, although he does not write out in his mind what is on the paper. He only nods after he reads it. Then Robert Day reaches across the desk and takes it back. A few nights later, Paul has Robert Day burn the paper with a Zippo lighter and put the ashes in a small glass bowl that Paul has Bonita bring into the office so he can look at her neck again and have her smile. However, after Bonita leaves, Paul notices that his Billion dollar paper has not been burned and that Robert Day crumples it and eats it. Robert Day does this on his own and Paul cannot not stop him.

By the end of the second week these scenes seem too much out of movies for Paul's dream, and so he returns to the version where Robert Day simply tells Paul of his Billion dollars, the phone rings on the table, and Bonita comes and goes with her neck and smile.

May I Come Over?

"Do you remember the time we dug the elevator hole?" said Lloyd. "For the new wing of the student center."

They were outside having drinks. It had stopped raining the day before and was in fact warm for April. Lilly has not yet arrived because Janet had asked Paul to come at five and Lilly at six. That way they could talk about the bookstore, and "other things." Janet has not told Paul who is coming. Lloyd doesn't know either. But he knows someone is.

"I've heard that story once too often," said Janet. "Not that I wasn't there. I want to talk about the store and other things."

"What *other things*?" said Lloyd.

"Other things," said Janet. "And I've heard that story a billion times."

"I just wanted to say," said Lloyd, "that you won't find kids today who would dig an elevator shaft hole by hand all night long to earn some extra money to buy books. I can't even get the boy down the street to mow the lawn for ten bucks an hour because he's in the mall on his cell phone. If he were reading Yeats under a tree to his Beatrice, that would be different. Or reciting Poe to the girls: 'Helen thy beauty is to me like those Nicean barks of yore . . . ' We dug that hole for four hundred dollars and split it four ways. Paul, me, Harris, and Baxter. Why we gave Baxter a share I don't know because he was always climbing out of the hole to talk to Dee-Dee. A hundred bucks to work from sundown to sunup. With two pairs of gloves, I still got blisters. And we broke three shovels doing it. You tell me the country hasn't gone to hell when . . . "

"What other things?" said Paul.

"Your life," said Janet. "And you," she turned to Lloyd, "might have climbed out of that hole once in a while to see me."

That night when he was putting himself to sleep, Paul returns to Robert Day's office and has Robert Day explain the conditions of getting the Billion dollars. First, it must be spent so that no one notices that Paul has so much money. Nor can he tell anyone. Paul can make for himself a life elsewhere where he can be as rich as he wants, but he cannot leave his job—although he can take more time off, go half time, or, after a while, retire early.

Paul must not make contributions to religious organizations. His benefactor is a "Free Thinker" and does not want any of Paul's Billion given to religious organizations no matter how worthy the cause may seem. Paul can make contributions (anonymously) to medical science, to the local college, the SPCA and other charities—but never to exceed a million dollars total a year. Also, Paul needs to consult Robert Day about any expenses over a million dollars. Or maybe it should be ten million dollars.

Finally, Paul is not to invest the money. The firm of Day, Schwartz and Whitehead will do all the investing and handle all the transactions. At present the Billion dollars is earning one million dollars a week and had been doing so for two weeks. Paul must spend both the earnings and the principle. This last stipulation seemed to come from Robert Day very much on his own. Are there any questions?

Just as Paul is about to say no, Bonita comes in with a tray on which are two cups of coffee and sweet rolls. She is wearing a black dress with white buttons down the front. When she leans over to put the tray on the table, she uses her free hand (her left hand on which there are no rings) to touch the base of her neck. She is wearing pearls. She looks at Paul. Just as when Robert Day ate the Billion dollar piece of paper, Paul has no control over Bonita's arrival, nor what she is wearing. But he likes the pearls.

Then the phone rang. Not in the office of Day, Schwartz and Whitehead, but beside Paul's bed.

"Hello?"

"Hello."

"Lilly?"

"Yes."

"What's the matter?"

"I wanted to tell you something tonight, but I didn't have a chance at dinner. May I come over?"

"Now?"

"Yes."

"Where are you?"

"At the store."

"So late?"

"Sorting books while I got up enough nerve to call you. 'Tinker Bell to Tolstoy.' May I come over?"

"Sure."

"Thank you."

There Was Less to the Eternal City Than Met the Eye

Until he began his Billion-dollar dream, Paul never read travel magazines: their prose was "not in the language"—to borrow a phrase from Lloyd. But more than that, articles on Rome seemed to be missing what was Roman. A magazine story on Piazza Navona would have it populated by leather goods shops and gelato stalls, but after fifteen hundred words and five color photographs there was less to the Eternal City than met the eye.

On the other hand, novels like *Don Quixote* or *Anna Karenina*—or recent ones like *Woman in the Dunes, Heat and Dust, Broken April*, and *Sheltering Sky* were to Spain and Russia and Japan and India and Albania and North Africa something of a projection in words. Cervantes and Tolstoy and Kadare and Bowles were place names that any decent map of the world should label along with Orwell, Infante, Sillitoe, Márquez, Bely. Instead of a shopping and eating guide to the Via Condotti, travel magazines would do better to reprint Joseph Heller's Roman scene from *Catch 22*.

Paul's book collection was arranged by country and city: The shelf for Africa had E. M. Forster and Lawrence Durrell, among others. Spain had Hemingway, Orwell, Lorca, and Laurie Lee. Paris went from Peter Abélard (recommended by Lloyd) to Émile Zola. Jean Rhys. Elizabeth Bowen. Mavis Gallant.

Because he had arranged his literary world to suit his geographer's world, it did not occur to Paul that he was missing anything by not traveling to the down-and-out-flats of London and Paris—much less to the grid of Petersburg. In fact, he seldom went anywhere.

"Philip Larkin, the English poet, rarely traveled," Lloyd had once remarked. "And Dr. Johnson said that grass is green wherever you find it. Or something like that."

She Wondered If They Might Be for Her

Lloyd was a poet and a printer. He taught at the local college. His printing business was in the basement of Books-and-Joe-to-Go. It was a letterpress operation: Chandler and Prices, a Heidelberg Windmill, plus two Vandercooks on which he printed limited edition poetry broadsides and posters for literary readings. He had made a decent living because he was an excellent printer and because Janet had a good sense of marketing in the world of small-press book collectors.

For the previous few years, Lloyd had been going to the store at night to print broadsides of his own poems: love poems written for a woman not named in the poetry.

Lilly knew about the poems because she found them one day when she was in the basement looking for an additional copy of Robert Day's reading poster that the author had wanted. She returned to the basement and, reading the poems, thought them not very good.

Of the ones Lilly read, all were frank expressions of desire. The poems imagined that the woman to whom they were addressed was responding in erotic ways: unbuttoning a blouse button by button per line, or revealing the *V* of her "essence" in the poem's closing couplet. But as no woman's name appeared in the poetry, Lilly did not know for whom they were meant. When she wondered if they might be for her, she stopped reading them.

You'll See

After Paul began putting himself to sleep with his Billion dollars, he stopped dreaming. He had always been quite a dreamer: wild, sometimes violent dreams with a large dark animal chasing him off the end of a pier until he falls into the water and then drowns to wake. Or dreams where he is endlessly on a rattletrap of a plane flying over water so low that it hits the masts of boats that break through the plane's windows. Sometimes sailors are tied to the masts. Sometimes there are fish that flop on the floor of the plane.

In another dream, Paul is on a series of trains going some place he is supposed to know, but there is nothing about the landscape (rocks and rills and open plains with few trees) that gives him a clue. A conductor keeps saying: *You'll see. You'll see.* And once Paul heard himself say in the middle of the night. *You'll see.*

"See what?" he had said to what he had said.

"Be quiet," Arlene had said.

Paul would awake from these dreams with the sensation of having survived. When he went back to sleep he would dream of tables of food and wine all set in a meadow with a silhouette of a young woman asking what he wanted most in life. Sometimes the young woman carried a book of poetry out of which she read aloud. When Paul awoke the second time it would be morning, and he could remember the young woman's voice, the food, and the wine—but not the poetry: nor what he wanted most in life.

"Between your talking and snoring, I don't get much sleep," Arlene had said. "I'm going to the guest room."

"What Did That Woman Buy?"

One day at the store, Paul caught a glimpse of a woman who looked like Bonita. She had the same blond hair and the same appealing figure. She had the same neck. For a moment he considered going over and asking if she needed help, but to see that she was not Bonita would be a disappointment. So he went into the office and put things in order for the literary event they were sponsoring that evening: a reading by a local poet. When Paul came out of the office the woman was walking down the sidewalk in front of the store's windows. From that angle she still looked like Bonita.

"What did that woman buy?" Paul asked Lilly.

"An art book on Goya and something else out of the sale bin," said Lilly. "*The Pillars of Hercules*, by Paul Theroux," she said, reading it off the cash registrar receipt. "They were both last copies, do you want to reorder?"

"I don't think so," said Paul looking out the window. There was a small silence between them.

"Have you put any more data into your life program about what I said the other night?" asked Lilly.

Paul noticed she did not smile, but instead looked at the floor. Nor had she put quotation marks around "data" or "life-program."

There. That Was Done

After Paul got his Billion dollars from Robert Day, and after they worked out the details of how he was to withdraw the money (through a special check card for amounts up to ten thousand dollars; by a direct payment from Day, Schwartz, and Whitehead for more; and by consulting Robert Day for expenditures above ten million), Paul began putting himself to sleep by devising ways to spend the money, and on what.

The night Lilly had come over, he put himself back to sleep by purchasing her three apartments in Paris and an English-language bookstore. The main apartment was lavish; the second apartment in the same building was for guests, and a smaller one for a maid.

When that did not put him to sleep, Paul bought the whole building and put the bookstore on the ground floor, and Lilly's apartment became the entire top floor from which she could see the Seine. There would still be the apartment for the maid, and one for guests, while the other apartments would be for visiting authors who were in Paris—either to give readings at the bookstore or to stay for a longer period of time (a year seemed about right). Lloyd and Janet would have a permanent suite of rooms in the building as well.

When all that buying did not put him to sleep, Paul established a foundation so that the writers who lived in the apartment could charge their meals at the literary restaurants in Paris. Any café or bistro or restaurant that turned up in Balzac, Proust, Baudelaire, Colette, Hemingway, Gertrude Stein, James Joyce, Genet, Jean Rhys and Mavis Gallant would be free to Lilly's authors. They could take their coffee on the first floor of Café de Flore, then get some chocolate at Debauve & Gallais to tide them over until they took dinner at Le Pré Catelan.

Paul calculated he spent ten million dollars for the apartment building (it would need some work and there was the furniture to buy—Janet could help with that—and the bookstore would need a stock to get it going), plus another ten million on the foundation. In all, twenty million. Not bad for a night's work. There. That was done. And so to sleep.

The next morning, while ringing up a book on investing, Paul realized that since his Billion dollars had been earning a million dollars a week, that even though he had spent twenty million in Paris the previous night, he had made little headway on depleting the Billion dollars itself. He remembered Robert Day had told him he must spend both the interest and the principle. But what would happen if he did not?

"Is something wrong," asked Lilly. She had noticed he had been standing with his index fingers on his brow for quite a long time.

"Not really," said Paul.

"I hope . . . "

"It has nothing to do with you," he said. And in the sound of his voice both Lilly and Paul heard an edge that had not been there before.

That night he decided to fly Lilly and Lloyd and Janet to Paris on the Concorde. Even though the Concorde was now out of service, he would buy one. What would a Concorde cost? Fifty million. Then there is insurance and pilots and maintenance, so there's another million a year. Now he was getting somewhere.

After the Concorde lands in Paris, Paul installs Lilly in her bookstore and establishes her among poets and writers—and in so doing he makes up for the edge in his voice. Which means he can return to Bonita. Which he does, buying her one of Gaudi's buildings in Barcelona and flying her there—also in his Concorde. But not on the same flight with Lilly and Janet and Lloyd. Paul sees these flights off at the airport: first Lilly, Janet, and Lloyd (whom he puts as the head of his Foundation, now that he thinks of it); then, two days later, Bonita leaves for Barcelona. Paul is standing on the tarmac watching her board the Concorde when he realizes he might never see her again. He tries to edit out the Concorde into which she is about to vanish. She waves to him. Paul cannot see if she is smiling or not. Then she is gone. Neck and all.

Beware of Great Wealth

"What would you do if you were given a lot of money?" Paul had said to Lloyd the evening Janet had invited him to meet Lilly. It was his way of stalling the talk Janet wanted to have about his life.

"Give it away," said Lloyd.

"All of it?" said Janet.

"Beware of great wealth," said Lloyd. "It is glass that shatters when it shines. And it never fails to shine."

"I'd want an apartment in Paris," said Janet. "Plus a second apartment in the same building so we could have family over. As long as we're into big-money dreams here."

"And maybe even an apartment for a maid?" said Paul.

"Why not?" said Janet. "I'd also buy a place in San Francisco. And go first class. On land and sea and in the air. It's too bad the Concorde has stopped flying."

"Give it away," said Lloyd. " Flee from both abstractions and money."

"Here's Lilly," said Janet as they heard a car drive up.

"Who?" said Paul.

"The rest of your life," said Lloyd.

She Looked at a Half-Empty Bottle of Wine

"Did I upset you when I came over?"

"No."

The store was closed and Paul and Lilly were cleaning up from the reception.

"I think something has changed between us," said Lilly. "I am sad about that."

"There's another woman in my life," said Paul.

"I wondered if there might be," said Lilly. She looked at a half-empty bottle of wine. "Will you share this with me? And talk. I don't mind if we are not lovers, but I would mind if I lost you in some other way. I promise not to ask any more 'provocative' questions."

Paul glanced at Lilly and wished he had not said anything about another woman. Unlike Bonita, Lilly was not pretty to him but in that moment when she looked at the wine bottle, tilting it slightly to see how much was left, he thought her lovely. What was there to do with that?

What It All Cost

Paul began reading *Flying* and *Yachting*, as well as *Condé Nast Traveler*, *Boating*, and *Millionaire Homes*. And decorator magazines: *Real Simple* and *Connoisseur*. Also magazines from Sothebys and Christie's; these—and many more like them—from the racks that a vendor filled once a week.

Paul saw what there was in the world to buy, the finest brands, and what it all cost. The *duPont Registry* listed the grand Peppertree Bend Estate, a sprawl of house that seemed to take up most of the 1.69 acres on which it sat: $7,199,000, which (Paul found himself thinking) probably meant he could get it for a flat seven million.

He made lists: Hinckley Sou'wester. $1.8 million; Gulf Stream IV, hangar in New Orleans, $5 million; the library of Montaigne at auction as well as a wine cellar from an English baron. What would they cost?

Paul could only guess. Montaigne at a million. Fifty cases of Bordeaux pre-1960 (including two cases of Mouton Rothchild 1945 and three cases of Latour 1938) at half a million. Paul put the lists into the office computer under: *The Billion Dollar Dream*. Then he hid *The Billion Dollar Dream* in the *Robert Day* folder that he had created when the author had come to read.

Beyond what there was to buy, Paul needed a place to live. Florida did not seem compelling, partly because he could not imagine who he might be in Florida: maybe somebody out of the movies like Jon Voight in *Midnight Cowboy,* only with piles of unexplained money. Maybe California: but who can you be with a lot of money in California besides a Dot-Com Somebody or a film star?

Perhaps in Europe or in Africa and the Far East, he could use the money to make of himself someone not Paul Andrews. But who? And then there was the matter of how to get there. He would have to give up his pleasure of not traveling. Life is a trade-off. These were problems for his nights ahead.

So What If He Had to Give Them Back

After Lilly had awakened him when she came over, Paul realized that by getting up in the middle of the night and putting himself to sleep a second time (and even a third time), he could spend more money. The best way was to drink two big glasses of water just before he went to bed. It was during these double and triple Billion-dollar dream nights that he began to buy islands and ranches and gold mines and finally, after some art books the store had ordered came in, hugely expensive paintings.

Not knowing what was for sale in the art world and impatient to get on with it, Paul imagined that various museums were selling off a few pieces of their celebrated art in order to finance their operations: the *Luncheon of the Boating Party* for sale by The Phillips Collection Gallery: fifty million. And as long as he was into Renoir, there was the *The Swing*. Another fifty million. For a week of nights he bought Della Francescas and small Leornardo drawings. Why not? He had an apartment building in Paris and one in Barcelona that needed furnishing. A few Elgin Marbles came on the market from a dealer in Kiev (no doubt stolen) and Paul snapped them up even if he would have to give them back. Five million dollars. Each. And there were ten. So what if he gave them back and lost the money.

Paul bought Francis Bacons, Gwen and Augustus John, Warhol's soup cans and his Marilyn Monroe (which he paired with a Joe DiMaggio), a fine southwestern painter Fritz Scholder, a whole family of Wyeths, some Catlins and Caleb Binghams.

Then one day looking through *100 of the Most Beautiful Women in Painting* there was Sargent's *Madame X,* and Paul saw that Bonita's neck was her neck. Before he fell asleep the first time (the painting might not be available later in the evening), he bought it. A hundred million.

By the end of the spree, he had purchased hundreds of millions of dollars worth of art. The next week he bought a building in Washington to house the American part of the collection. Twenty million. After two weeks of two and three glasses of water a night he'd finally made a big dent in the Billion dollars. It put a spring in his step at work; a sense of accomplishment. The weather was getting warmer; it would soon be May.

"She's Lovely, Isn't She?"

"You cannot leave the money to anybody when you die," says Robert Day. "Nor can you invest in houses. That is, you cannot buy them unless you plan to live in them. Nor can you be discovered living in them by your friends or family. Nor are you allowed to pay off your mortgage, nor the loan on the bookstore. If you get married, you may not let your wife know your secret wealth, although you can treat her lavishly. Buy her minks and diamonds if you like. Which brings me to this: I have learned you bought an apartment building in Paris for one of the women employees in your bookstore. And for another woman, you made a similar purchase in Barcelona. As I said at the beginning, you cannot reveal in any way to your friends, your associates at work, your relatives, your would-be-lovers that you are a wealthy man. No Paris apartment for your store employee. No flying off to Spain on the Concorde with some woman just because you think her neck is pretty. And no buying paintings that are not for sale, and never will be. Return the paintings. Sell the buildings."

Bonita comes in with her tray of coffee. She is wearing black slacks and a yellow blouse in which her breasts jiggle. As she leaves the room, she turns toward Paul and cups her hand at her waist and makes a movement not unlike someone snapping castanets. She smiles.

"She's lovely, isn't she?" says Robert Day.

"Yes."

"She's my daughter."

Once Robert Day says that, Paul could not rewrite it. No matter how many times over many nights he tried. But later that night, and night after night he could—and did—change the rules against buying Lilly Frame an apartment building in Paris as long as she did not know who did it, and he fixed it so he could buy Bonita the Gaudi building in Barcelona—again as long as she did not know the source of the gift. And he also fixed it so the paintings (*Madame X* among them) need not be returned; but still Paul could not rewrite:

"She's lovely, isn't she?" says Robert Day.

"Yes."

"She's my daughter."

What Do You Think about before You Go to Sleep?

"Would you really not accept a lot of money if it were left to you?" asked Paul. He and Lloyd were in the basement of Books-and-Joe-to-Go.

"How much money?"

"As much as you want."

"You mean if I won the lottery? A hundred million or so just last week. Would I turn that down?"

"Yes."

"No. But I'd be wrong not to."

"Why?"

"See this?" said Lloyd holding up a sheet of paper.

"Yes."

"It's a love poem. A single sheet of a love poem. I wrote it. I set it. I printed one copy. On paper I made myself. Then I distributed the type. It's unique. I've done twenty of them. They are dedicated to a woman I love. I don't really love her. It is just that I need somebody to love other than Janet. Let's call her Lilly. Just like Lilly upstairs. Or Arlene. Like ex-Arlene. Or

Dee-Dee. Are the poems good? Not as good as the other poetry I write myself, which I think can be pretty good. But better than Rod McKuen. At least that. Our Lilly is my Beatrice Portinari. Your ex-Arlene is my Dark Lady. Dee-Dee can be either Helen or Hera; I prefer Hera even though Helen was more beautiful. But then there is the problem of Zeus." Lloyd looked at Paul. When Paul didn't say anything, Lloyd continued:

"We all need something to imagine, and then we need something to do with what we imagine. I am not a great poet because my love for Lilly is not great, and it is not great because I do not see her circa 1290. In my mind's eye I cannot make her die young. She is not an ox-eyed beauty. She is not even the poet inside of me, which is who I think the Dark Lady was to Shakespeare. The love and woman of my poems are weak illusions. But at least they are *my* weak illusions. My inner eye is making what I want to see. A poet is a seer and a maker. Got it?"

"What's this got to do with the lottery?" said Paul.

"Money steals you blind. It is one thing to be Milton or Homer or Borges; it is another to have an eye full of getting and spending. Even as is, I have too much of it. Janet wants to dig a swimming pool because we have the money. And we're not talking by hand. I drive a stretch Volvo. I have IRAs and 401ks and Janet has a money counselor. By now on my best days I've got cataracts. If I took a hundred million dollars from the lottery what eyesight would I have left to see Lilly Frame as Beatrice? Or me as my own Dark Lady? I'd have only money. It's a rotten deal. Having enough may be too much if you want to be a poet."

Lloyd put his poem on the job case.

"You know that Robert Day who was here a couple of months ago?" Lloyd continued. "The one who read a story about a crazy populist rancher in the middle of Kansas with nothing but short-grass prairie and blizzards. Day had it right when the old rancher tells his banker son that time's not money it's 'gossamer.' Nothing is money if you have it. It not only steals you blind, it steals your time. And you need time to breed lilacs out of desire."

There was a long pause in which Paul found himself thinking in bits and pieces: old maps; the tight binding of new books; Bonita's neck; the conductor saying *you'll see, you'll see*; Lilly that night she came over; Janet, an afternoon long ago; the lovely woman who read him poetry and kept asking him what he most wanted in life; two sets of washers and dryers; and *behind that line lie all the capitals of ancient Europe*, Paul said aloud. Or thought he did, but probably not, because Lloyd said:

"What do you do with money anyway? Buy boats. Apartments in San Francisco like Janet wants to do—and where, coincidentally your ex-wife lives, as I happen to know but Janet does not. What else? Planes. Cars. Swimming pools. How about I buy everything that is advertised in the *New Yorker* in one of those big fat issues that comes out just before Christmas? Everything. A week's worth of 800 numbers and emails. That would start the little, brown attic-stuffer truck driving up to the house three hundred and sixty-five days for a year. Then when the house is full I'd rent stuff-storage-sheds, or—here's an idea—I could buy houses all over the country: beach houses on both coasts and the Gulf of Mexico; *Lord of the Flies* islands; Peter Fonda ranch houses in Montana; *Up in Michigan* lake cottages; Santa Fe adobe houses out of Willa Cather—all so I would have some place to put the little-brown-truck-attic-stuffer-*New Yorker*-stuff." Lloyd picked up his poem off the job case.

"But you said you'd accept the money," Paul said.

"Yes."

"Because of Janet?"

"No," Lloyd said. He was reading his poem to himself.

"Why?"

"Why what?"

"If you wouldn't accept the money for Janet's sake, why would you accept it?"

"I'd accept it for you," said Lloyd looking at Paul. "So you could run off with Lilly Frame, if that's what you want to do."

"That's not a straight answer."

"I'd take it because I am not gifted enough to imagine not taking it," Lloyd said looking at Paul over the edge of his poem. "And it would ruin my life and I would know it every night I go to bed and don't put myself to sleep imagining Lilly reading the poems I have written to her and don't imagine her doing what she is doing with her buttons and her body as she reads them. I may not love her, but I want to. What do you think about before you go to sleep?"

Paul's Dream Was Stuck

Paul's dream was stuck. He had bought nearly everything in the magazines that came into the store, as well as islands and ranches and boats and planes and wine cellars and Bentleys and, in fact, all there was in the recent *New Yorker*. He had run out of ideas. And where to put everything was a problem just as Lloyd had predicted. Maybe he could buy a town.

"What kind of town?" asks Robert Day.

"Some town in Kansas."

"With people in it?"

"I would buy them out. To get their houses for everything in the *New Yorker*."

"I don't think so," says Robert Day. "But there is something else you need to know."

"What?"

"The money is earning two million a week."

"Even with what I spent?"

"Our investments in hedge funds have paid off very well. Two million a week and maybe more by the end of year. You're filthy rich. Get used to it."

Bonita arrives with coffee. She looks even more lovely and younger than on previous nights: she is wearing a dark blue dress cut just above the knees. A small, white ribbon is pinned to her hair. Paul is about to speak to her, but she seems distant. Maybe she's unhappy in Barcelona. Maybe she's taken up with someone else. Lloyd? Whatever the trouble, it takes Paul a long time to get to sleep lying awake thinking about what Lilly had said to him both the night she came over and later when they finished off the wine. Then there was what Lloyd had said, and finally in the background of his mind a thought that seemed like an elevator moving up and down slowly out of which came a voice saying: *You'll see. You'll see.*

He got up and went through the living room to the kitchen and poured himself a glass of milk. He looked in the trashcan, then at the clock on the microwave: 10:12. 10:13. Then he picked up the phone and called Lilly.

"Hello."

"Lilly?"

"Is that you Paul?"

"Did I wake you?"

"I was just reading."

"I'm sorry to have bothered you."

"You haven't really." There was a moment of silence, and just as Lilly was starting to say something more, Paul said:

"Are you coming to work tomorrow?"

"Yes. Of course. Why do you ask?"

"I don't know," said Paul

"Is something the matter?"

"I'll talk to you tomorrow," said Paul and hung up before he could hear what Lilly was saying.

Later that night Paul tries to see Robert Day but Robert Day is not in. Nor is Bonita. The building is there: tall and full of glass with marble floors and a spacious elevator that takes him to the top floor. But when Paul comes into the offices of Day, Schwartz and Whitehead, there is nobody. He goes back down to the lobby and into the street where he meets Robert Day, but when Robert Day speaks he sounds like Lloyd.

"I want to give the money back," says Paul.

"You can't," says Robert Day whose face is the face of Arlene.

"Then I won't spend it," says Paul.

"Fine. We don't care if you spend it or not. But each month we will still send you an accounting. When it reaches ten Billion you die. Or maybe it is five Billion. I'll have my daughter check the contract."

"Where's Bonita?" says Paul.

"She went to Paris with Lloyd."

"Aren't you Robert Day, the writer?" asks Paul.

"I used to be," says Robert Day who is now sounding like the train conductor. "Who are you?"

"I'm in love with your daughter."

"She's gone to Paris with Lloyd," says Janet who is suddenly standing in the street holding Robert Day's hand. "She's taking off her clothes to the beat of poetry. Button by line. Her blouse is off."

"He's dead at five Billion," says Bonita, who is nowhere to be seen.

When Paul awoke, the clock read 4:23. He could not get back to sleep even though he tried by having the woman who read him poetry and poured him wine come into his head so he could tell her what he wanted most in his life, but she would drift away as if she were not, after all, interested. Then Lilly and Janet showed up, but they had become fat and old and the head of Lilly and the head of Janet had switched bodies and in that way they both talked to him in Spanish about washers and dryers. Finally, Paul got out of bed and went and sat in his car in the driveway until the sun came up.

"I do not have another woman in my life," Paul said to Lilly Frame later that morning.

She was shelving in the cookbook section.

"What happened?" she said.

"She left me."

"A house with two sets of washers and dryers," said Lilly, "is like having your pie à la mode with the ice cream on one plate and the pie on the other. Or like dividing Czechoslovakia in half, which they should have never done because who wants to buy a travel guide to the Czech Republic and then another one to Slovakia?" She smiled. But only slightly. And it seemed cautious.

"I am sorry I said you were 'provocative,'" Paul said.

"But I was," said Lilly. "I want you to be in love with me the way I am in love with you."

"No two loves are alike," said Paul, rather surprised that he had something so interesting to say. And in his mind's eye he saw Bonita.

"That's what your brother says."

"He does?"

"It's a line in one of his poems. The ones he prints downstairs. I think they are meant for me."

"I didn't know about them until the other day," said Paul.

"Some minds think alike," Lilly said. "Here." She handed him a copy of an Elizabeth David biography.

"What's this?"

"It's a new book we got in. Two copies. It doesn't mean anything that I handed it to you; it's just that I'm nervous and don't know what to say."

Neither one of them spoke for so long that both of them thought the other one would soon say something.

"How about we go downstairs and open a bottle of wine that I've got in the office and I'll read my brother's poetry to you?" said Paul. Again, he was surprised at what he had said. At its audacity.

Lilly was silent for a moment. She looked at the floor.

"I'd rather not," she said and went to the front of the store to check out a customer.

Arlene Was a Sorority Sister of Janet's

It had been while digging the elevator shaft hole that Paul met Arlene. Arlene was a sorority sister of Janet's. Once, when Paul climbed out of the hole to get some water and to start lowering the bucket to get the dirt out once the hole got too deep to throw it out, there was Arlene. She asked him if he'd like something to eat, because she'd be glad to run to the Food Shack. Paul was the only one of the four of them who did not have a girlfriend and he learned later that Janet had arranged for Arlene to show up. After that, Paul and Arlene dated throughout college and then married.

But they almost did not get married because of a conversation between them a few weeks before the wedding: Arlene asked Paul if he had ever slept with anybody and he lied and said no. Then Arlene asked if he had ever wanted to sleep with anyone and Paul said of course. That was natural. Then he thought he better not lie to Arlene because that would be a bad way to start a marriage, and so he told her he had slept with two women: one was a prostitute the fraternity had hired for a bachelor party and one was another girl. When he wouldn't tell her about the second one, Arlene said she was going to call off the wedding. So Paul said she was his high school girlfriend and that her name was Bonita. In fact it had been Janet. Janet had asked him over to her apartment before she dated Lloyd and when he went there she was naked to the waist, saying come on, hurry, hurry. They were lovers until she took up with Lloyd. But not after that.

It never seemed an important lie. Nor had Janet ever mentioned the matter. Nor had Lloyd, if he even knew. But just now, seeing Lilly at the front of the store, the memory of that lie blinded Paul's mind. What he wanted most in life was to tell Lilly the truth—not only about the lie he had told Arlene, but the story about Robert Day and the Billion dollars, and how he had made up Bonita for both Lilly and Arlene, and that Bonita had not left him because she was never Bonita in the first place. He might not be in love with Lilly Frame, but what was there to do with not being able to see what to do? But Paul said nothing. Later in the day Lilly asked if she might leave early that afternoon, and Paul said yes.

That night Paul tried to put himself to sleep by thinking of Lilly Frame and what it would be like for the two of them to be married, and how they would live in the house together, and what Christmas would be like with his children and Janet and Lloyd—and maybe even Arlene, if it came to that. But in his mind's eye he could see none of it. The best he could do was get a Christmas tree in the living room, but it had no lights and there seemed to be nobody in the house. Not even himself.

Next, Paul imagined the countries he had studied as a student. A flickering Albers Equal-Area projection came into his head but when he tried to put in Armenia or Ethiopia or Goa, or a town in Kansas, it vanished. Next he tried a stereographic projection, and for a moment he could see Cuba and the edges of Mexico and Central America, but maybe it was the sea coast of Albania. As for the Mercator grid he finally conjured, there was nothing in its boxes: not seas, not plains, not mountains, nada. No matter what view of the earth Paul tried to imagine, it was not there. Nor were his books. No Rhys or Forster. No Mavis Gallant or Colette. Paris was gone.

Later that night, Paul went back to Robert Day's office. He was going to say he wanted out of his Billion-dollar dream so he wouldn't have to spend the money or die. But when he got to Washington, the city was gone. There was only the vast short-grass prairie through which the train in his nightmare traveled.

He tried to see Bonita. He tried to hear her voice. He tried to have her say *I love men who take their coffee black*. He tried to smell her, to have the pearls string down between her breasts. But in so doing even the short-grass prairie flickered and vanished, and finally there were tiny dots and now and then a reddish vertical band. He opened his eyes and turned on the light, then closed his eyes again to see what he could see. A pale nothing this time, but still nothing.

"You'll see," he said out loud. "See what?" he said to himself, again out loud. He turned off the light and with nothing to put him asleep, he lay awake for hours until it was morning. He stayed in bed while the phone rang and he could hear that Janet, then Lloyd and, yes, Lilly Frame, all left messages wondering where on earth was he?

Robert Day's short fiction has received *Best American Short Stories* and Pushcart Prize citations. Among his awards and fellowships are National Endowment to the Arts, both Yaddo, and McDowell Fellowships, a Maryland Arts Council Award. His fiction has appeared in such places as *TriQuarterly, North Dakota Quarterly,* and *New Letters*, and his nonfiction has appeared in *The American Scholar, Washington Post Magazine, Smithsonian,* and elsewhere. He is the author of the novel *The Last Cattle Drive*, a Book-of-the-Month Club selection, two novellas, *In My Stead*, and *The Four Wheel Drive Quartet*, and two short story collections, *Speaking French in Kansas*, and *where i am now*. He has taught at the Iowa Writers Workshop; University of Kansas; and Montaigne College, University of Bordeaux. He is past president of the Associated Writing Programs; the founder and former director of the Rose O'Neill Literary House; and founder and publisher of the Literary House Press at Washington College where he is an adjunct professor of English literature.